DECEIT

DECEIT

A NOVEL

Yuri Felsen

Translated by Bryan Karetnyk

ASTRA HOUSE ∧ NEW YORK

This is a work of fiction. Names, characters, places, and incidents are products
of the author's imagination or are used fictitiously. Any resemblance to actual
events, locales, or persons, living or dead, is entirely coincidental.

Astra House
A Division of Astra Publishing House
astrahouse.com
Printed in the United States of America

Library of Congress Cataloging-in-Publication Data

Names: Fel'zen, I︠U︡riĭ, author. | Karetnyk, Bryan, translator.
Title: Deceit : a novel / by Yuri Felsen ; translated by Bryan Karetnyk.
Other titles: Obman. English
Description: First edition. | New York : Astra House, [2022] | Summary:
    "Set in interwar Paris and taking the form of a diary, the novel relates
    the complex and fraught relationship between an unnamed narrator and his
    love interest and muse, the beguiling Lyolya Heard. Subtle and profound
    in its exploration of love, deceit and betrayal, Felsen's novel is a daring
    and highly original work of psychological fiction"—Provided by publisher.
Identifiers: LCCN 2022021755 (print) | LCCN 2022021756 (ebook) |
    ISBN 9781662601965 (hardcover) | ISBN 9781662601972 (epub)
Subjects: LCGFT: Diary fiction. | Psychological fiction. | Novels.
Classification: LCC PG3476.F43675 O2613 2022 (print) |
    LCC PG3476.F43675 (ebook) | DDC 891.73/42—dc23/eng/20220622
LC record available at https://lccn.loc.gov/2022021755
LC ebook record available at https://lccn.loc.gov/2022021756

First edition
10 9 8 7 6 5 4 3 2 1

Design by Richard Oriolo
The text is set in Bulmer MT Std Regular.
The titles are set in Bulmer MT Std Display.

Contents

Foreword

On Saturday, February 13, 1943, a crowd of 998 men, women, and children clamber out of the dilapidated boxcars and down onto the *Judenrampe*, the unloading platform for new arrivals at Auschwitz II-Birkenau. The transport has been organized by Adolf Eichmann's department of the Reich Security Main Office, which is overseeing the deportations of foreign-national Jews from occupied France. This is the forty-seventh such group to make the two-day journey from Drancy, a transit camp situated in one of Paris's northeastern suburbs. En route, three people—two men and one woman—tried to escape but failed.

It is the sabbath, and among the crowd, a tall, elegant, slightly stooping figure, noted for his "Aryan" good looks and fair though graying hair, joins the men's queue, awaiting selection. For those sent to the right, what lies in store is registration, tattooing, disinfecting, and, ultimately, hard labor in the typhus-ridden camp. For those sent to the left: death. Though the figure, whose documentation lists his profession as "*homme de lettres*," is only forty-eight, the SS doctor examining him notices his slight stoop—the result of an affliction affecting the ligaments of the vertebrae—and duly directs him to the left. That night, a little after the sabbath ends, the figure, along with 801 others, is led off to one of two bunkers that lie to the north of the ramp, converted farmhouses hidden from view by woodland. We cannot be certain whether it was in "the little red house" or "the little white house" that he met his end (although it was most likely in the latter), but we can be sure that late that same night his body would be borne out and disposed of in a nearby mass grave.

Yuri Felsen's death plunged him into near-total obscurity. Flight from Soviet tyranny early in life had put him at a significant disadvantage, obliging him to ply his Russophone art in European exile. Writing "difficult" prose and being labeled "a writer's writer" had sunk his chances for posthumous fame lower still. His death was followed by the mysterious disappearance of his archive, and so, in addition to what he published, only a handful of his papers survived and now scarcely any photographs of him remain. And yet, here was a man who in his heyday had been held up alongside Vladimir Nabokov as one of the more gifted and distinctive writers of the young Russian diaspora, an author who had embarked on one of the most ambitious literary projects undertaken in Russia Abroad, an artist who, despite deep artistic divisions in the emigration, had achieved something miraculous: accolades from every quarter and faction (and, perhaps most astonishingly of all, from Nabokov himself). According to

Georgy Adamovich, the doyen of Russian Montparnasse, Felsen's prose "left behind a light for which there is no name"—and indeed, for all that fate tried to efface the man, he made an indelible, if now faint, mark.

Felsen was born in 1894 in St. Petersburg, the then-capital of the vast Russian Empire. However, if you were to search in the archives of the city today, you would find no record of any such individual, for his real name was in fact Nikolai Freudenstein. The eldest son of a distinguished Jewish family (his father was a doctor and his extended family held influential connections at Court), he was a brilliant student who won a coveted place to read law at Petrograd Imperial University, graduating in 1916, as he would later claim with a mix of irony and self-deprecation, "without the least vocation for it."

In the wake of the Bolshevik Revolution, he and his immediate family fled to Riga, in newly independent Latvia, where he soon made his first forays into print, writing feuilletons for the local press. Keen to "rejoin" Russia, however, he journeyed on in the summer of 1923 to Weimar Berlin, a city abuzz with cultural renaissance and hyperinflation, and then, toward the end of that same year, to Paris, the self-styled capital of the diaspora. Settling there, he engaged in what he archly termed "independent ventures" (which is to say he dabbled in the stock market and illicitly traded foreign currency). He likewise wasted little time ensconcing himself in the literary scene and, having metamorphosed into the *littérateur* Yuri Felsen, promptly set about launching his career as a writer in earnest.

He debuted under his artfully ambiguous pseudonym in 1926, but it was the publication of *Deceit* in 1930 that consolidated his reputation as a serious writer. It was this work, moreover, that marked the first step in a grand literary opus that would, by the time of his death, encompass two further novels, *Happiness* (1932) and *Letters about Lermontov* (1935), as well as seven interlinking short stories, each of which develops the project episodically, jigsaw-like, all the while advancing the same long-suffering hero's romantic, psychological, and artistic evolution toward his literary vocation.

Taking the form of a diary, *Deceit* presents its readers with a sustained psychological self-portrait of a young Russian émigré, a neurasthenic and aspiring author whose oft-thwarted amorous pursuits of the elusive Lyolya Heard provide the grounds for so many beautifully wrought extemporizations on love, letters, and human frailty. In its opening pages, readers—like voyeurs, party to the unnamed diarist's most intimate thoughts and burgeoning infatuation—accompany him as he goes about the city of his exile, making enraptured preparations for the materialization of his fantasy, revealing not only his eagerness, dreaminess, and poetic inclinations, but also his compulsive desire to analyze his surroundings and self. Yet as the bright optimism of the opening passages gives way to darker emotions, these ravishing, beguiling flights of scrutiny soon betray subconscious slips, solipsisms that hint at his more monomaniacal tendencies, which at times blind him, for all his sophistication of thought, from the true nature of his circumstances. So begins an exquisite game arranged by Felsen, wherein it falls to the reader, while delighting in the narrator's observational acumen and linguistic bravura, to second-guess the essence of what really lies behind those descriptions, and to plumb the depths of deceit in all its manifold variety.

The baroque, tortuous prose style that Felsen contrived to give expression to this elaborate counterpoint of thought, emotion, and subliminal motivation immediately distinguished his voice from any other. "Whosoever reads his works will agree," wrote Adamovich, "that they contain poetic vision and psychological revelation. You cannot confuse them with any other book." It was, moreover, the combination of this unique style with the novel's psychoanalytical motifs and its intense focus on a love affair whose cruelty fuels the narrator's creative faculties that justifiably earned for Felsen, as Marc Slonim recalled, the epithet of *prustianets*—a Russian Proust.

Yet while Proust and his philosophy of love, art, and jealousy may figure most conspicuously among Felsen's artistic models, *Deceit* has at the same time a broader eye on the literary fixations of its day. On the surface, at least, the novel resonates with the leading literary genre of the diaspora: the human document. Confessional, deeply psychological, drawing copiously on autobiography, the movement prefigured autofiction by almost half a century: militating for the documentary at the expense of fiction, it sought to make an art of the author's own reality. And sure enough, the narrator's self-portrait in *Deceit* broadly accords with what is known of Felsen's own biography: the dissipation of a life spent in exile; the drip-drip of economic precarity and the eternal pursuit of money; the engagement in various commercial enterprises and obscure "independent ventures"; the string of romantic liaisons crowned by an impossible love affair with a married woman who appears and disappears with tormenting regularity. Yet while Felsen may share all of this with his fictional narrator, he is careful to keep them on parallel tracks, never letting their lines cross. For a diary, the work is remarkably short on specifics. We never learn, for instance, where or even in which part of Paris the narrator and the object of his romantic attentions live. Though the work is strewn with all manner of cafés and restaurants, not a single one is ever mentioned by name. It is only by circumstance that we deduce the lovers' first encounter must take place at the Gare de l'Est. Indeed, all the expected particulars of day-to-day life—details of work, money, acquaintances, the narrator's very habits and modus vivendi—are more often than not traduced only to what immediately touches on the mercurial and enigmatic Lyolya, who, as she is glimpsed from every angle and distance over the course of the novel, forever remains the epicenter of the narrator's psychological and emotional world.

By obscuring these details that would otherwise tether the work to its time and place, Felsen goes beyond the human document as such, discarding the ephemerality of the mundane to look unswervingly beneath, at the hidden workings of the psyche. Stripped thus of its topicality, this timeless work of diarizing an individual's inner world—hinted at so elegantly by the discreet omission of the date's final digit in the very first entry—propels the novel beyond mere documentary and even led one perceptive critic to view the work not so much as an exercise in deceit so much as a study in the possibilities of truth itself.

Though it may seem frivolous to have written of love in years so bleakly marked by a darkening landscape of social upheaval and political polarization, of proliferating fascism and fanatical communism, years in which the émigrés' dreams of a return to Russia were dashed irrevocably, it would be a mistake to think of Felsen's art as the product of a nostalgic romanticism. For him, writing his latter-day *ars amatoria* was as timely as it was urgent; it was an act of political defiance, one that sought to reaffirm the supremacy of the individual in an age when ever-newer regimes were forcing more and more private citizens to submit to the collective. "I do not know to which movement to ascribe myself," Felsen muses in an autobiographical fragment. "I should like to belong to the school that . . . for me represents a kind of neo-romanticism, the exultation of the individual and love set in opposition to Soviet barbarism and dissolution in the collective." Refusing to enter into dialogue with brutes, he instead developed a writing that was antitotalitarian in essence, championing love, artistic freedom, and individuality, and seeking to give them rich, lucid expression at a time of political pressures that would sooner deny them, at a time when so many of his contemporaries were desperately seeking out new ways in which art could provide adequate response to mounting tyranny.

The power of art to defend the humane was an article of faith to which Felsen clung to the end. On the eve of the war that would ultimately rob him of his life, he responded to critics who, in those dreadful years, maintained that it was no time to write of love or sentiment, of individual need. "I cannot fight directly—my sole act is that of observation," he declared, "but we are defending the same thing, man and his soul." For him, this was the ne plus ultra of art in exile: "Everything that ought to be said about the writer's role in our terrible and absurd times pertains doubly to the literature of the emigration: the emigration is a victim of non-freedom and, by its very raison d'être, a symbol of the struggle for the living and of the impossibility of reconciling with those who murder them. Its literature must express this 'idea of emigration' with twofold force: it must animate the spirit and protect man and love."

Ultimately, Felsen's belief was not enough to spare his life. Nor was it enough to save the real-life prototype of Lyolya, his

Beatrice of Riga, who shared in his woeful fate, dying in the Shoah in Latvia. Yet in spite of all this, his art remains. In the Talmud it is written, "Blessed be the one who resurrects the dead." I hope that in raising him from obscurity I can do the next best thing. And what better place to begin than his art, which, for all that has been lost and destroyed, shall forever be the truest testament to his life.

Deceit, then, or truth? Fiction or fact? Perhaps it would be more fitting if we imagined the novel as a fictional palimpsest written over the now scarcely legible lines of Felsen's life, one in which the most vital, transcendental details can yet be glimpsed. For those willing to look and weigh each in the balance, there is surely much truth to be found in his *Deceit*.

—B.S.K.

Translator's Note

Yuri Felsen's *Deceit* was first published in Paris in 1930, more than a decade after its author fled Russia. The novel is, in many respects, a product of his exile—particularly of his Parisian years. When he arrived in the French capital from Berlin on New Years' Eve in 1923 (after an arduous experience involving several days' travel and a run-in with the Belgian gendarmerie), we might imagine that he heaved a sigh of relief. The journey, he explained, was one that had "breathed with hostility toward the traveler, one in which hidden dangers had lurked at every corner." Yet, despite the ordeal, his optimism remained undiminished. Like so many of his fellow stateless refugees, he had been seduced by the promise of this latter-day Shangri-La: those were the days, he recollected, when nobody yet suspected that Paris would be "overrun with Russian restaurateurs, chauffeurs, and dressmakers, who even themselves had no inkling of their calling."

For most, however, those initial hopes gave way to disenchantment soon enough, as the fantasy was dashed against so many bureaucratic nightmares, cultural barriers, and fast-dwindling public sympathy for their plight. In the end, the comfortable lives that they had envisaged in the Third Republic were often reduced to those of poverty and humiliation. Indeed, by the time that *Deceit* appeared, their economically precarious and peripatetic existence had become notorious, encapsulated in the never-ending succession of down-at-heel boarding-houses, or *pensions*, through which they would roam (as do Felsen's characters), and which had already become an emblem and a literary cliché.

While Felsen rarely allows these tenuous practicalities of exile to encroach on the psychological landscape of his prose, they do inform many of the assumptions made on the reader; hence, a few words are in order, to aid the modern reader's orientation. Like Felsen himself, the unnamed diarist in *Deceit* is engaged in business of some kind, although the precise nature of the diarist's enterprise remains eternally obscure. It is clear, however, that he works in some irregular capacity for the wealthy Monsieur Derval, and that in so doing he has managed to escape the more "penurious misfortunes" faced by so many of his fellow émigrés; nevertheless, he still lives from check to check and must endure spells of "worrying—with indignity and gall—about every little expense." That he can spend his evenings idling in the cafés of Paris is not a marker of relative prosperity, but rather evidence of the more affordable drinking culture of the day.

If the narrator has avoided the embarrassment of the "guardsman-turned-chauffeur" cliché, Lyolya and Ida Ivanovna share in another archetype of émigré experience: the dubious dream of working in Paris's fashion industry. Although not the "mannequin with a title" of Monsieur Derval's fervent imagination—that is to say, an aristocrat-turned-model (the corresponding cliché for formerly privileged women)—it seems likely from the context that the samples of Lyolya's "Berlin work" shown to Derval are in fact designs for garments (making her eventual refusal to sew the narrator's glove even more pointed). Of all the Russian characters, Ida Ivanovna has ostensibly made the greatest success, becoming the owner a milliner's atelier. But this success is tinged with sadness; her professional accomplishment has come at the private cost of perpetual loneliness, and even her being is "stripped of her nationality."

While much of the narrator's day-to-day life takes place within the Russian enclave, he appears to operate with ease among native Parisians, engaging chance acquaintances in cafés and often eavesdropping on their conversations. (Indeed, it is the overheard invective of the mustachioed Frenchman at Blainville that reveals so unambiguously the negative shift in public attitude toward Russian expatriates.) And while Felsen's narrator may boast an appreciation for the culture of his host country—he consumes contemporary French novels, admiring André Maurois while having trouble with André Gide—he has a more complex relationship with the French language itself. He is impressed by Lyolya's calculated show of her "excellent French pronunciation," yet he scorns his rival Bobby's "clueless Gallicisms," all the while seemingly oblivious to his own, not infrequent, Russianizing of French turns of phrase—a consequence, we assume, of his many years spent in exile. To preserve these dynamics, all the original French of the novel has been retained, and some supplementary phrases added, to echo the narrator's own idiosyncratic *métissage*.

p. 17 *Non, je me défends toute seule*: "No, I look after myself."

Aï, aï, aï, quel cataclysme: "Ay, ay, ay! What a tragedy."

fille de la rue: Lit. "girl of the street," i.e., a streetwalker or prostitute.

p. 32 *peut-être j'en suis trop éprouvée*: "Perhaps I'm too long in the tooth for it."

p. 51 *C'est épatant*: "How marvelous!"

p. 52 *Mais elle est charmante . . . et bien tranquille*: "But she's charming, your friend, and so very meek."

p. 69 *L'amour supporte . . . la trahison*: "Love endures absence and death better than doubt or betrayal." A quotation from the novel *Climats* (1928) by the French author André Maurois.

p. 93 *comptable*: "bookkeeper."

p. 98 *fausse-forte*: "deceptively large."

p. 125 *de cinq à sept*: Lit. "from five till seven," a French expression denoting the hours between finishing work and returning home, traditionally a time reserved for lovers' trysts and extramarital affairs.

p. 134 *Et votre amie, qu'est-ce qu'elle est devenue?*: "Whatever became of your friend?"

p. 135 *mon cher, voilà*: "There you have it, my dear."

p. 165 *quelle veine vous avez*: "You're in luck!"

p. 166 *un peuple mérite . . . lâches*: "A people deserves the regime it gets. For you Russians, it's Lenin, or Ivan the Terrible . . . Just look at those people who surrounded the poor tsar, they all abandoned him. They were all cowards, cowards, cowards."

du meilleur monde: "a cut above."

p. 181 *bilan*: "balance sheet."

p. 202 *madame descend tout de suite*: "Madame will be down shortly."

DECEIT

PART I

E VERYTHING I HAVE is superficial—appointments, acquaintances, timekeeping—dull and dry, and it hopelessly anesthetizes what little in me remains alive, my final frail impulses: I cannot achieve even a melancholy clarity with regard to myself, a sense of remorse, however inert, or the simple warmth of human kindness. Only more persistently than before, more shamefully, do I sense that I am the same as others, that, like everybody, I will down idle days in trivial anguish, and that one day I must, as must everyone else, rightly disappear. Throughout my years of loving tenderness and incessant jealousy—covetous, hasty, though never apt to bear a grudge and quick to forgive—I had, in a sense, greater magnanimity, would blithely turn my back on those sinister and terrible comparisons (with "everybody else"), on the absurd inevitability of the end, and considered my own sublime sense of nervous tension unique. Now, however, when all this comes back to me every so often—limp, numb, and impoverished—and afterward follows a period of deep, somnolent repose, I succumb to an error one so often descries in people—that the present will never change—and so I conclude: my sense of romantic exaltation has ended once and for all, as have all my private thoughts and feelings, but in such moments, so reflective of the past, one need only seek to discern something, to uncover it and communicate it—for the remnants of those emotions, of that exaltation, are preserved, that old anxious haste no longer interferes with them, and perhaps their bothersome recollection, which painstakingly reconstructs what was once achieved but has now been left behind, constitutes the entire sense, the whole bizarre purpose of these lonely and wasted years. But then, no sooner does a sliver of blissful, inane hope appear—from a touching similarity, a smile, attention paid to my words—than in an instant I alter, no longer do I see my present humdrum rut, and I forget that all these private thoughts and feelings are over, and only my obstinately suspicious nature—that vestige of experience, failure, and the eternal attribution of value to everything—unexpectedly and opportunely sobers me: but then suddenly comes despair or treachery all over again. Or else in the wake of sobriety I experience that belated, blistering, vainly defiant sense of regret, which sometimes brings women (seemingly without provocation) to tears—because of the opportunity to have something rare and dangerous, something that was meant to be, and because now that opportunity has been lost irrevocably.

I suddenly felt this opportunity for something blessed, dangerous, and new as I was reading a letter from a Berlin acquaintance of mine, Yekaterina Viktorovna N., who has written to inform me that her niece, Lyolya Heard, is coming to Paris—"Remember our conversations about her? Help her, look out for her—you surely won't regret it." Katerina

Viktorovna, a colonel's widow, a faded army woman cut from a hulking, much too masculine cloth, and possessed of a coarse, gray face and a booming wooden voice that manneredly gave commands, would for days on end, in the Berlin *pension* in which we had found ourselves cast together, regale me with stories of her beloved niece, "a rare, exotic creature, quite unlike any of these local girls," whereupon she would smile boastfully and suggestively, with just a touch of sympathy, as it were: "That's her, my darling—what a great pity you haven't met her." These were still desperate times—the last of money, candor, and hope—and that aging, destitute woman, herself bereft of hope and prospects, compensated herself with this fantasy of a romance between her beloved pet and me—in some measure I conformed to her naïve and sentimental martial notions of chivalry. Not only did she try to allay her insatiable womanly kindness by offering up in her own stead the equally attentive, lovely, and clever Lyolya Heard, but she even tried to reconstitute a scattered, vanished social circle, the little bit of influence she was used to wielding, the conditions in which Lyolya and I could meet, in which Katerina Viktorovna could aid and abet us. At first, I did not credit her bombastic raptures, but there were photographs, letters, casually uttered words—each of them drew me in more than the ingenuous praise of the old colonel's widow. In turn, I, too, constructed an image of Lyolya Heard—a dazzling, delicate blonde with an inquisitive and cultivated mind, vulnerable and at the same time courageous, able to tackle any setback head-on. I recall in particular her hands in one of the photographs—elegant, capricious, clasped awkwardly, as though in despair, but unyielding all the same. Lyolya Heard, in leaving her husband, had found herself alone in Belgrade, unable to move to Berlin, and when at long last she did move, I was already in Paris.

December 8

S HE ARRIVES IN five days' time. By then I shall have clarified a small matter that will allow me several months' freedom from having to seek out new ventures, freedom from worrying—with indignity and gall—about every little expense, freedom from putting off necessary purchases (collars, shirts, neckties). The crucial thing is that it will make life easier and more pleasant when I am with Lyolya, about whom I am beginning to think with rapture and hope: even now I want to show her around Paris, to take her out, to entertain her, not to begrudge her time, not to think that somewhere somebody is waiting for me and that I must brace myself for the negotiating table, not to let up and forever be reminded— money is vital, how good it is to have it.

Why does the knowledge that Lyolya Heard is coming here so captivate and uplift me? For so long I spared absolutely no thought for her whatsoever, but something strange and unhealthy began back then, that day in Berlin—because of her, because in her person, inadvertently, so to speak, two wills collided, two desires that were equally intense, alien to one another, having originated long ago and for reasons that are very likely unclear even to me. I shall attempt to master my mental inertia and put a name to these reasons, to combine them, to wrest them from their mute dormancy into which everything that befalls us plunges, unmarked at the time—I am sufficiently practiced in such acts of remembering, and I have a presentiment (perhaps artificially fabricated) that something brand new is about to commence with Lyolya's arrival, which means that my old—especially those old—associations with her must be tidied up and put in order. I am glad even that between this mysterious last minute—here, in this room, in this solitude—a minute yet blind and merely conjuring Lyolya's arrival, that between this and her first friendly smile at the station in five days' time, all those wearisome tasks will be carried out before the feast, whose purpose is to prepare me for some great happiness, to prepare me not morally, but mentally—rather a submission of accounts than some regenerative Hindu act of purification.

Those two wills—mine and Katerina Viktorovna's, sympathetic muses that befriended one another unexpectedly—were powerful, each in its own cause, for they transported us both to what was most immediate and vital: above all else Katerina Viktorovna feared being torn from the past, feared seeing herself as "some old colonel's widow," gray and haggard; she wanted to appear girlish, younger, blonder, svelter, when really, since her youth, back home—there, where she had once been listened to—men had courted her, reckoned with her, and so it was not my presence or charm that imparted to her this illusion of youth, home, and the continuation of her former life (although it was from her that I received the affectionate little nickname "the romantic youth"), but rather the attention, genuine, avid, and rapt, with which I listened to her when the talk was about Lyolya—obsessively I wanted one thing only: to find myself a "Lyolya" just like this.

Like many people who have once upon a time found and then lost what they desired, I was far from any thought of embarking on some immature, ill-defined search and knew perfectly, ad absurdum, what it was that I wanted, what sort of woman, setup, and relationship I would pick. Very likely my first condition would be to exclude any docile, dewy-eyed, excessive youth, that there be no need to "educate" her, to remake her in my own image, only then to look, as into a mirror, and with ennui recognize myself (if successful), while also risking the misfortune of some rude and spiteful surprise. I have always wanted not only to offer support, but also to find a support—a friend, an opponent, an intellect, a force—and not on account of weakness, but rather because of some (granted, inconspicuous, not even wholly conscious) hubris, so that there come about a fascinating, daring contest, a comradely and romantic union, on equal terms, instead of a swift and foolish takeover, so that my partner already be on the same spiritual plane, rarely attained by women, where everything dignified and precious, everything characteristic of love—mutual reliance, ennoblement, support—becomes, for both parties, deserved and assured. Such emotional depth in women, one that rivals my own (or that which I ascribe myself), is the vestige of experience, struggle, happiness, and failure, and is in no wise the result of a miracle: I have had girlfriends, spoken with people toward whom I knew unhesitatingly I might have been able to direct my long-standing readiness to love, so jealously guarded and unspent—but each time I would stop myself (this ploy will work at first) because of a lack of money, because of my habit of waiting for one last, irresistible "next adventure," which would usually never come to pass. Yet Katerina Viktorovna somehow managed to inspire me with the notion that this unequivocally irresistible "next adventure" was none other than Lyolya Heard: I succumbed to the infectious excitation of a lonely woman in revolt against fate and old age (though her excitement had more to do with herself than Lyolya), and insensibly credited her arguments in Lyolya's favor—true, they were casually uttered and superficial, but they moved me by having some sort of correspondence with the very thing for which I had always been searching, and in which, without that decisive push from someone else, I feared to believe. These superficial arguments, which I understood perhaps arbitrarily and which I modified so that they would please and convince me, consisted in Lyolya's shrewd maturity, in her pains to seek out worthy individuals, in her indifference, mercilessness even, toward those who proved unworthy, in her struggle with poverty, in the recent calm, uncomplaining help—considerable, stalwart, at times self-sacrificing—she gave her husband, without any of the usual people around to console her, people who turned out to be petty and malicious (as, incidentally, did those whom she consoled); all this, imaginary or real, overfilled me with the hope that Lyolya was in some way destined for me, that she, too, would be sure to choose me and place me among those few who shared in her human (if one can put it thus) significance, and I relished the anticipation of this, envisaging myself—reserved, not apt to "poke my nose in"—suddenly exposed by Lyolya's perspicacity, and so not for the first time in recent years, with the impatience of a beggar awaiting a legacy, I took to counting down the empty days that passed by in idle expectation. Occasionally, the insipidness of this hope would become too much (I recall many a time in Berlin when I would suddenly cool toward Katerina Viktorovna's words and tales, once so arresting, and hear her out half-distractedly, with a strained civility, and in her frustration she would dub me not "a romantic youth" but "a diplomat"), yet each time my rapid disillusionment would turn out to be nothing more than the statutory poststimulation crash and my old trust, my old feverish hope, would return to me. Once again, I have been preparing for my anxious first encounter with Lyolya, and in her alone I continue to see a resolution, an end to this dull, drawn-out tract, something inimitably luscious, overwhelming and impossible to defer, something I once possessed and which has forever remained a beguiling, exhilarating reflection, an irrepressible "belief in love."

I AM OFTEN put out of sorts by the fairly commonplace notion that every expectation will be frustrated, that the joy proclaimed to us will be robbed—and not only by absence of mind, unconsciousness, or sleep, but also by the trivial, routine necessity of work, into which we must plunge ourselves without trace. Thus, I know even now that in advance of Lyolya's arrival much preposterous scurrying about lies before me, much loathsome, mercenary unrest and odious effort required to hear out rejections with composure, to persuade afresh and with skill, and I know that this will eclipse both the blessed joy of anticipation and that other task, about which I wrote yesterday—that of tidying up the past, outwardly pointless, but worthwhile even so.

Now I am faced with that devastating, depersonalizing period, when with every ounce of quivering tension you are drawn to one thing only, to success (as you sometimes are at cards or the races), because you need it, because it is your salvation and because it is foreseeable to the point of clairvoyance; that is why every moment you rebuke yourself for inaction, you want to prod someone, to mend something, and almost superstitiously you fear rest or repose. I fancy that I find initiating business inherently more difficult—like any beginning it is hard, but the difficulty also comes about because of the insulting uncertainty of my situation: I emerge from somewhere in the ether and must practically truss myself to both ends of the affair, neither of which has any need of me—and often, fearing ridicule, not wanting to become a petitioner, I delay for weeks on end the decisive first conversation, in suicidal quiescence, like those petrified during a terrible dream or before some deathly waking danger. But even if that first jolt into action comes uneasily to me, a time like the present, when the principal obstacles have been eliminated and all that is left to do is wait for the money, with impatient avarice, fearing that other obstacles may arise yet— such a time is somehow even more torturous: no longer must you, as at the very start, break and harness your will, but then nor is there that conventional posture of dignity and correctness (it would be too obvious a fall), and every failure, no matter how small, every new restraint, is grimly borne—to the point of exhaustion.

For all this neurasthenic fever of mine, so flagrantly base and self-interested, I find sundry justifications. I ascribe it to an aptitude for commerce and rejoice—it means I shall not perish. I ascribe it also to my lengthy penury, to the odious trivia that remind me of it (they are many: the morning selection of a shirt and the far-from-comic despair that they have all turned to parchment with age, the obligatory dash past the concierge, with the haunting suspicion that she can see me through the wall and rightly despises me, the over-cooked muck served up in the restaurant and the dismal beer in the café, the dread of running into those lovely people who had placed their confidence in me, or of engaging seductive and easily known women in conversation)—regarding each piece of trivia like this, I try to believe that I am, for the last time, standing on the threshold of some miraculous change, but then, after some hiccough, some obstacle, some failure, I find myself at once on the threshold of nothing, do not believe in rapid change, deem myself fated to vagabondage or beggary and am ashamed of my deceived friends, of the dinners at somebody else's expense, of my comfortable bed in my unpaid room, of all that hopelessly absurd life, which imperceptibly leads me to despair and savagery. This would appear to justify my feverish pursuit of money—in my usual industrious state I cannot even conceive of its absence, I disburse and allocate it in advance, and for me such precipitate assuredness is not some empty, accidental fiction: much of what I have initiated has already paid off, and, each time it did, I rejoiced anew, astonished that here, in Paris, having relied on both family and the state, I should now be feeding myself, paying for my (albeit modest) desires, and, in the trappings of a mid-range restaurant, taking for granted the waiters' servile attentions. But the fact that money is so humiliatingly vital, and that its appearance is very likely, even imminent, still does not excuse, does not expose that darkest, most disturbing part of me, which I am utterly unable to get at: it is an arid inferno, isolated, removed from everything external, a never-ending fear that sprang one day from that ungodly money, a fear that became, with time, abstracted and void (it swoops down in oddly silent, ever-quickening bursts, making it impossible for me to dwell on anything, to concentrate, to recollect myself)—and never shall I comprehend, never shall I bring to heel this barren, destructive flame. And yet, for the first time it has failed to engulf me entirely: something gentle and ennobling—from love's anticipation, from joy at the prospect of Lyolya's arrival—will remain forever, and I can discern, almost graphically, how diluted, how diminished by the other are each of my two overflowing "passions"—and perhaps that is precisely why I can take both of them in my stride.

December 10

THE DEAL IS in the bag: were I not so suspicious— owing to many misfortunes in the wake of certainty and naked achievement (which are chalked up to bad luck, and for that very reason are so especially galling)—I should think that there could be no doubt about it, and that tomorrow morning I need merely go and collect the money. Yet now, after this wealth of experience, my aim still seems beyond my reach, it seems as if the affair is dragging on and will be decided only tomorrow, the moment I receive the money, and for now I must once again set aside my schoolboy glee at this resounding victory, at impending leisure, as well as that other glee—for the first time absolute and unencumbered—

concerning Lyolya, and must somehow pass the day that is so like unto those that came before it.

I continue to deny myself every little trifle; in the café I drink, instead of a liqueur, always the same insipid beer, although I have no trustier means of making myself insensible to time than swift, stupefying inebriation, and although I know *ex ante* how readily and recklessly I shall spree from tomorrow morning. Granted, I am never outright lavish or extravagant—each of us has our own unwritten rules, our own elastic limit of expenditure, which depends on circumstance—mine is somehow too prudently linked to the duration of the result: it will seem natural to me to spend a whole evening in an expensive venue and not to go home in a taxi, because the journey shall pass in an instant—as you set off, the end is already within reach. But even that is not quite the whole story: I have an additional fear of "useful purchases" that purport to bring long-term benefit; I have that terror of "big numbers" peculiar to those without a steady and guaranteed income, to those whom "big numbers" much too graphically hasten toward penury, toward the bewildered, long-familiar question: where do I go from here?

But all this austere "codex" (it is less consistent than presented here) will be thrown out the window and forgotten the moment I find myself in somebody else's company: accidental words from any quarter, an unexpected appeal, will lure me to help, pull at my heart strings, compel me to give some parting assurance of support, and not one that is insincere but made good—throughout years of solitude, there has amassed in me sufficient unspent, muted *tendresse*, and often it is directed at people like me, but who are more helpless than I am, and incomparably more frequently at women for whom I have even the slightest partiality. This is probably connected to yet another, intimate reason for my irrational profligacy: I have the unhappy knack of being determined too much by women—as a student at the *gymnasium* I could not, at a ball, "off-load" a dull young lady I had invited to dance, and would await liberation from her, so as not only to rejoice in freedom, but also to take pleasure in pitying myself, the jilted party (thus, as it were, forestalling my amorous lot)—and so now, having at last attained an indifferent, grown-up invulnerability, if in a café I should unwittingly engage in conversation my plain, painted neighbor, I will not resolve to stand up, leave, and suddenly disappoint her, but find myself compelled, like some *naïf*, to squander my money on her.

Such was the case even today: almost against my will, with a semiabstracted gesture, I invited to my table in a cheap, lively café a rosy-cheeked young girl who was playing an animated game of cards with her girlfriends; when she came over, I scarcely succeeded in tearing myself away from the imaginary novel (a romance) that ordinarily fills my quiet hours, and managed after a fashion to keep up the necessary pleasantries until I was stopped in my tracks by a single turn of phrase (uttered sweetly and with dignity, I thought); I wanted to help, but recalled at once that this was impossible, that it would rob me of the time I had just calculated I needed, and all this I explained to her awkwardly.

The words that had surprised me were essentially run-of-the-mill (to my enquiry about a boyfriend, she replied: "*Non, je me défends toute seule*"); it may well have been her tone of voice that transformed her into someone new and respectable, yet there is something impossibly refined in that ready Parisian patter, which lays equal every social group (perhaps with the exception of the "intellectuals," who are, as they are to the majority of Russians, unknown to me) and so reconciles them that there is little to distinguish between my new acquaintance and that debonair old boy from the wealthiest of families, on whom my affairs depend and who, at every mention of our penurious misfortunes, of these guardsmen-turned-chauffeurs, of these mannequins with titles, exclaims with indignity and distress: "*Aï, aï, aï, quel cataclysme*"—both the viability of such a comparison (a gentleman for whom wealth was a birthright and a common *fille de la rue*) and the miracle that the common girl off the street has imbibed these artful turns of phrase and that infallible, unerring tone, perplex and move me necessarily.

Reading over today's page, I am astonished—yet again—by how much of my writing, owing to my dogged pursuit of accuracy, is sharper and more intense than what I think and see, and by how little correspondence there is between such "accurate" entries in my diary (though scrupulously faithful, they are condensed by the weight of the words and by my inexplicable determination) and my initial vague observations. Granted, there are also things that go quite unnoted—among these is the imaginary romance, which I am now describing for the first time, about which I find it strange to think in habitual words and definitions—so much is it all outwardly delicate, mute, disembodied. I concocted it at the age of sixteen, when I experienced those first impatient, jealous forebodings yet to be augmented by experience—which kills imagination (now made redundant)—and with some sort of stubborn indolence I lugged it through the entirety of my youth, through adventure and experience—strange and unique, like everybody's—changing but little of the original according to my later hopes and desires. For years I have been recounting to myself these same pleasant details during rare hours of quiet wrested from the tumult of business, from amorous woes and recollections: this "romance" is my repose, a constant source of release and oblivion, and because of this I do not hear, I do not notice words, I do not even catch the ends of phrases and, thus immersed, I delight—for I am telling of myself, as I would want to be, as I am imperceptibly becoming.

These polished, familiar details and their half-melancholic serenity alternate with stirrings for Lyolya—stirrings whose authenticity I immediately recognize and which spill into absolutely everything, irrespective of what happens to me throughout the day: they acutely influence not only the "romance" and my foolhardy fever for money, but also my scatterbrained curiosity out of doors and the poems (mellifluously lulling or unexpectedly wounding) I read aloud at home—and so every experience of the day leads me just as naturally to Lyolya; how hard it is to tear myself away from them for the sake of some rarefied and drearily calculated diary entry, which today seems (perhaps because of Lyolya's imminent arrival) particularly dead and dry.

December 11

I RECEIVED THE money this morning, and it, having saved me from horrid, degrading poverty, from the imperative of limiting myself like a beggar, from spiteful and sorry bitterness (had I been thwarted), from everything unpleasant and drearily repugnant—this money, as it were, unveiled and exposed Lyolya to me. I am an appreciative, perhaps even deliberately appreciative, sort—indeed, is it not better, more dignified, simply more advantageous, to rejoice in success for days on end than to be conceited and hardly mark it at all?—time and again I expressly remind myself that it is good to mark success modestly (being rare, it is a good thing), how much worse things could be, what impediments have been avoided, what perils have left me fortuitously unscathed. I also wish to demonstrate to myself that this joy is not a sigh of relief from a neurasthenic after some drawn-out, slipshod, half-abandoned job, but rather the just satisfaction that is granted us as the fruit of our success—and that if a sudden new obstacle were to present itself now, I should be prepared at once to set again to work and struggle. The latter is especially true, but my readiness to struggle and work is born of will—standing in contrast to my inherent aversion to any form of labor or exertion—whereas the joy of completion, of looking back, is perfectly neurotic and lazy, and all my painstaking determination is probably little more than the vestige of ambition, of the deadly drive to perfect (as though for show) anything and everything, of the inherited practice of submitting loyally and without complaint to any duty or order, albeit imposed from without.

Opting not to stop at home, I set out posthaste for all the shops that I required—earlier, before the money's arrival, in order not to tantalize myself needlessly, not for anything would I have lingered by a shop window (much too enticing and beyond my reach)—today, however, as soon as I left the "bureau," where the debonair old boy had paternally slipped me a primed envelope containing a check, I immediately began totting up how much I would spend on what, adjusting the figures, swapping one decision for another and proving to myself once again that I was quite able to make spontaneous decisions—indeed, I even drew up a half-mock (though quite earnest) budget, carefully adhered to it, and then hastily bore off my purchases, so as to lay them out together all the quicker. At home each purchase seemed to me a miracle of good taste (as we find everything that bears the hallmark of our selection, our accidental favor, our slightest efforts, and to which we immediately cede both our sense and our serene equanimity), and each of these tastefully chosen items, gifted to myself, unexpectedly drew me closer to Lyolya—for her sake alone had I chosen them, and so in every respect, even in this act (not only mentally and emotionally), did I prove myself worthy of her.

The day passed almost without note and with less anxiety than I had anticipated—but between it and tomorrow's arrival there is still night, oblivion, sleep, which, more than strenuous and dull work, makes any event seem farther off: the expectant consciousness only distracts itself in work; in sleep it vanishes completely. This is why I am more indifferent toward death than most people: how much more dreary effort, how many more nocturnal vanishings until it comes— and then I shall die, not the man I am today, throbbing with life, determined, but that unfathomable new man, the one I shall become—perhaps in the distant future—after all the bothersome distractions that still await me.

Toward evening a telegram arrived—"MEET ME TEN A.M."— bringing with it that former impatient anxiety of mine, which now began to flourish, betokening a feverish insomnia—I wanted somehow to ward off the expectation, to make its transition into dream easy, to half-lull myself to sleep and thereby artificially expedite the morning, yet, in order to make a record of this in my exasperatingly meticulous and sober mind, I also wanted to "revel in my success," or, to be more precise, to revel in the fact that everything had come off so uncharacteristically smoothly—without the usual postponements and obligatory unforeseen obstacles.

I brace myself momentarily and step into a smoke-filled and drunken mid-range Russian restaurant, where, deafened by the quick-paced music, the ceaseless flickering of the waiters, the array of elegant and provocatively inquisitive women, the unfamiliarity of such fast-moving, vibrant images, I lose all sense of myself, my ungainly, restless legs, my now-limp body, and I look around hopefully, thinking how I might sit more conveniently so as to see every one of these women at once and leisurely select from them a few particularly attractive ones—to exchange glances, to get to know them (hardly likely, of course), but mostly to practice tenderness, to hold imaginary intimate conversations, which since childhood (true, now they are distinguished by a rather different tenor, one lacking that former ardent credulity) I have constantly and secretly carried on.

The table that fell to me was most unfortunate—right in the middle of the room—and so I found myself with my back to several young women, whom I had scarcely glimpsed but already marked, and now, as far as I was concerned, they had vanished, casting those left into even greater relief, much as other people vanish, potential friends or lovers—at a railway station, at a street corner—and others yet who truly are dear to us, if they end up spending some considerable time in an inaccessible foreign city. But then, for them, we too vanish, effectively making way, abetting others, as it were; and yet, rather than console us, this should only remind us once again of the irregularity of human relations, of their dependence on the most insignificant trifles, which so obnoxiously evolve into destiny.

In order to shrug off the burden of anticipation entirely, which had been allayed already by the restaurant's balmy air, I drank several double measures of vodka in quick succession, feigning that I was not in the least drunk and, by dint of my forgetfulness, amazing even myself, for ordinarily I do not get drunk at once; instead, I become unrecognizable and find myself unable to hold back the change. This time, the change that came about was astonishing, and, what is more, there was seemingly no transition: all of a sudden I succumbed to a gay impulse, one that was beyond my control, as though inspired from without, that was ever-quickening and thus drew me toward it more and more inexorably, so much so that the usual disappointment in the wake of sobriety could never follow it—and I trusted the lusty, frenetic, emancipated music, striving not to listen, not to think that it was all a sham (even with its now saccharine, now violent Rumanian accompaniment), and rushing to catch up with its gasping, rapturous—so unlike anything of my own—flight. Admittedly, the music was encumbered by the food—because of the vodka, and perhaps on account of my restraint, the pies and rissoles seemed particularly delicious; it is not often that food makes me wax lyrical, rather it constrains me outwardly, which dims my enthusiasm on occasion as well: what with the exposed way in which we eat, how unabashedly carnivorous we must seem, our noble, self-sacrificing decisions (though stimulated by the restaurant's music) are at odds with this, and in cases like today's, I hastily devour my favorite dishes, which are delicious (down to the very last morsel), and then, with counterfeit inattention, as though already in thrall to some noble or bitter emotion, I refuse what is left on the plate and ask for coffee to be brought—a cup of coffee imparts a certain (to my mind, worldly) finality to what is, for me, the endlessly fascinating pose of a quietly drunk man, as he poisons himself more and more and pours the most merciless scorn on himself.

But now the plates have been cleared away, the cup of coffee sits before me, and inwardly I can relax, while outwardly—maintaining a serene respectability—I only hint at the exalting, dazzling effect of the music and the reminiscences it provokes, and, using this cue and my own (apparently unusual) self-control, I somehow impress and intrigue those glittering worthies I selected at the outset, when I walked in, whom I continually follow with my gaze and who also (with unrelenting application, but in that feminine way, vain and surreptitious) observe me from various tables. My drunkenness is most often narcissistic: my usual uncertainty vanishes, my opinion of myself, of my success, increases to the point where it blinds me, I become intuitively enterprising, ignore obstacles, recognize no fear, and should be glad of a fire, danger, panic, only to cut a dash with my daring for all to see; when suddenly a long familiar melody will bring me to recall my true past, at times sorrowful, hopeless, suicidal, and then this sense of the past, magnified tenfold by all that I have drunk, will be charged with that same fastidious, narcissistic pride, and perhaps the only alternative is a form of drunkenness brought on by despair, a rare thing in these humdrum years.

No longer do I consider, as I once did (after my initial observations and contentious, hasty conclusions), that a drunken obsession is especially edifying or capable of revealing something new and inspiring—the mind grows unmistakably feeble, many of one's memories (be they detailed or shaky) are erased, what is set down in the heat of the moment later proves to be insignificant and rambling—and yet there is something genuine, albeit senseless, in inebriation, a lack of self-pity, the facility of adventure or sacrifice, a kind of brash and vulgarizing power.

I mixed liqueurs, dissociating myself more and more, taking leave of myself and, in so doing, almost participating in the general harmonious flight—of the music, of the crowd's heavenly smiles, which promised kindness and devotion, and of the song's careless, unduly expressive lyrics: as the old Gypsy woman sang, dressed in her low-cut, modish, anonymizing dress, she seemed to be trying to instill in these strangers her potent, passionate sounds by force. Her voice reached me with a sort of captivating power, communicating, precisely and succinctly, what had taken place within me, and this was adorned and enriched further by her singing—many things seemed to have deluged my memory for good, troubling me, affecting me, forcing me to challenge myself and to clarify something about myself ardently and in honeyed tones. In the composed, sober light of day, those same lyrics may seem naïve, limp, and devoid of their pie-eyed sorcery, but so irresistible is this sorcery that the words lodge themselves in the memory along with all their oft-repeated pleas and protestations. Now the Gypsy woman urgently sings out my favorite "everyone remembers their beloved"—and, one after another, muddled thoughts race through my mind: that without fail "everyone" will remember (there is a touching grandeur to the enormity of the generalization); that I too shall remember is, for me, the most important thing, but these words refer not to the past (though the music might easily have awakened that), but to tomorrow's Lyolya, in sudden proximity, alive and almost palpably in love with me. Then comes a new, dance-like, lulling meter and new, peculiar words—"the heart is spent on caresses"—they have the charm of a humble, uncomplaining, eternal readiness to sacrifice, but my objection is unwavering: no, the heart is not "spent," but enriched—one need only crack open the heart's riches and they shall prove inexhaustible. A man's ingratiatingly solicitous voice continues softly: "*I* shall leave you as I did before, proudly, though they will think you are still mine." I find myself inadvertently envious: never have I been able to command such favor—those whom I selected, oblivious though they are, would laugh at me, and they have long already convinced me that it can be no otherwise, that it cannot be amicable.

Opposite me is a Russian *danseuse* (she will dance with men for money); she looks just like the others I singled out—the ones who have been tormenting me, or who could torment me—practically naked, a strawberry-blonde with an intelligent, if somewhat impertinent face. That cherished, fixed state of contemplation, which I usually hold to be saturated with life and naturally creative, seems impossible to me; because of the music and the memories, because of the affordability of this woman, I want to reach that crude, perhaps real, life all the quicker and gift myself a night of unencumbered generosity. Yet my grown-up better judgment, coupled with never-forgettable experience, warily stays and sobers me, as if counseling me not to spoil Lyolya's arrival with ridiculous and shameful trifles—ill-humored fatigue, some absurd disease, at very least the fear of taking ill. Without any effort whatsoever, I cheerfully master myself, because Lyolya's arrival is definitively upon me—and the anticipation is impetuous, easy, and augurs well.

December 12

I RESERVED A room not far from my own, in a cheap and relatively clean hotel, and set off for the station to meet the ten o'clock train from Berlin. I set out late, so that I should not have long to wait, dawdled along the way and, having learned that the train was delayed, and surprising even myself, slipped out of the station and ran across the street to buy some flowers. I picked out some deep-crimson roses—dewy, fresh, still in bud, with unnaturally straight, wire-supported stems—and this bouquet was the first thing that transported Lyolya from imaginary life into reality, the first point of contact between my feelings for her and my physical self, a pledge of kindness (of sorts) that immediately bound me to a new and unbroken logic: thus do all our poignant, prevailing attitudes to people—enduring loyalty; unselfish, self-sacrificing solicitude; sweet, simple attention—often begin with some random, capricious act; then do we find ourselves guided by various half-conscious motives (tenderness to ourselves, a penchant for the gratitude of others, a fear of disappointing, sometimes an intolerable and tedious sense of obligation), which yet fortify our charity but bear hardly any relation to the original cause—doubtless, many of us cannot recall why we tip the waiter in one café double that in another, though we still consider ourselves duty-bound not to alter our preference. Such an original cause, one that necessitated my tender affections for Lyolya (now a given), was found in these fragrant morning buds, which by rights, owing to our nonacquaintance, I should never have brought, and it was these (as I was writing only a moment ago) that inadvertently revived the habitual chivalrousness of my long-excited thoughts about Lyolya, securing her with a well-intentioned, effective, earthly act, after which her physical appearance could no longer be anything new or unexpected, or abruptly interrupt my former candor toward her, and so it was that all this strange preparation, begun by Katerina Viktorovna, sustained by a feeble, half-desiccated imagination of twilight years, and then stimulated by five days' anticipation and yesterday's good fortune, led to Lyolya in the flesh—forgoing the inevitably dangerous interim of space in which to think rationally, of scrutiny and disenchanting comparisons.

Amid the slow-moving, unwieldy crowd of arrivals, among the first to arrive, I recognized Lyolya by her ermine stole and dark blue overcoat, which I had been informed she would be wearing, and yet I should have recognized her all the same—she was just as Katerina Viktorovna had described her and as I myself had pictured her for years: she has an uncommonly pale face (as though from too much powder), eyes that resemble a doll's—on account of their porcelain-blue hue and her long, heavily sweeping lashes—and (after all this, as it were, artificial stiffness) an unexpectedly sweet, pursed, quivering smile. Lyolya is slight and a little below average height, but, for all that, she holds herself upright, with movements that are so exquisitely well-defined that she seems tall and strong. Without the least hesitation I approached, encouraged and uplifted by the absence of anything new, by my continuing readiness to serve. In the taxi we talked about Katerina Viktorovna and Lyolya's eyes smiled good-naturedly, soothingly and with a certain calm assurance: I know about you and you know about me—how good it is that we are together now. From the very outset Lyolya was more assured with me than I was with her, though we were each of us equally prepared for the other—thus sometimes a boy, declaring his love for the first time, is for some reason more embarrassed, more anxious than his equally inexperienced coeval. What was more, I immediately divined in Lyolya a particular knack for people and conversation, one characteristic of so many independent women, a gift for talking to anyone: she understood things intuitively, would reformulate her questions to clear matters up at once, and effortlessly made those shameful, ordinarily veiled and essentially friendly remarks, without which human intimacy remains forever difficult and hopelessly tentative. The room was not to her liking:

"Forgive me, darling, you've been terribly kind and helpful—how often Auntie said you would be!—but you're trying to make an impression with all your thoughtfulness and you aren't thinking about how to arrange everything properly. I'm only saying this to you—not for myself, but for the next time—I don't mean to reproach you even a jot. Quite the contrary, I haven't yet told you how touched I am by all this."

In the end, however, the room was not changed:

"It seems we're going to get acquainted, you and I. Why should I hole myself up so far away from you, when it's probably better suited for me here. Only tell me frankly, I won't be getting in your way, will I? You aren't just being too darling, are you?"

With a fair degree of precision, I detected curiosity and trepidation, the vague feminine desire to infer something and not to have any competition—for all my doubts, I can now detect the faintest, most hidden partiality for me and, though I say nothing, I am touched. I immediately allayed Lyolya's fears, and no longer does she doubt my firm friendship; for my own part, I trusted in the benevolent correctness of all her advice, let her decide things for us both, and imperceptibly it was established that she will somehow protectively take the lead in everything. Her various judgments impress with their insight—of a kind that makes you blush and is not so frivolous as mine—such unerringly intuitive simplicity, for me, is much more persuasive than any far-fetched and inaccurate complexities. Not only does Lyolya divine others' thoughts, but she seeks out her own, even if they are unflattering, and freely owns to them; this comes out naturally, gaily even, without any pitiful or lumbering sense of self-reproach. I struck up a conversation so common among people of Lyolya's and my age (thirty and over), people who find themselves alone but still hopeful—a conversation about a misspent youth, about a time when there was a love that shook one forever:

"These are the only riches you and I share; it's the only thing that makes us interesting to each other and, if you will, close to one another. A strange 'capital' for our 'partnership'—as though it doesn't belong to us, but is purloined. But it isn't worth being embarrassed or keeping quiet about it—after all, it's all we have."

We proceeded to discuss how Katerina Viktorovna was getting on. I decided not to mention the fact that I had recently helped her. Lyolya was already aware of it, however.

"Your discretion isn't as laudable as you think. Admit it, you want to be found out more than anything—then you'll be victorious without having spoken so much as a word. It's the same when people hold back some important or good news, only to surprise people later on with their restraint—it's all because of vanity, which is an absurdity among friends. I don't value or much care for such excessive restraint—*peut-être j'en suis trop éprouvée.*" (Lyolya has excellent French pronunciation.) "Let's judge each other on merit."

Lyolya's manner of speaking may be described a little oddly (though without any contradiction) as "restrained candor": candor in the sense of a certain directness, an unflinching acknowledgment of failure, a lack of embellishment, calculation or false, ostentatious modesty; and a restraint that expresses itself to the same degree, in some shamefaced, impoverished adjective, in a sort of niggardliness of description. I like Lyolya's voice—it is deep and a touch monotonous, but sometimes warm and convincingly melodious.

We spent practically the whole day together and Lyolya told me a great deal about herself. She listens to me attentively, patiently (freezing comically in concentration), but after her brief, pointed, condensed stories, and after various eloquent answers, my words sound false somehow. Ordinarily, I envy those with the capacity for happiness, people who do not have to try, and yet I accept Lyolya's all-encompassing success as if it were my own, and even this morning I admired the unfalteringly graceful dexterity with which her sweet, capable hands tidied the room and then mended for me a new glove that had come apart at the seam, whereafter she proffered it to me, wincing at my excessive gratitude. Late in the afternoon I remembered (or, rather, I "remembered" only insofar as Lyolya was concerned, whereas in actual fact I decided this very morning) that I must tell her about last night's restaurant and how much better it would have been had she been there with me—and all the more vividly did I envision how irresistibly I should have gravitated there. Lyolya agreed readily and, with a smile that verged on tender, said:

"All right, but I refuse to bankrupt you anymore and I have no money for going out. After tomorrow, our 'outings' will be frugal and friendly—and, please, you mustn't get cross or try to dissuade me."

Soon I must go and fetch Lyolya (she is getting changed at her *pension*), and for the first time in a long while I have no worries, not a single troubling or tedious presentiment, no desires aflame with impracticability, and it seems almost certain that what is to come will also be like today—good fun, carefree, uncomplicated.

LYOLYA WAS WAITING for me, feverishly preoccupied in front of the mirror, and she seemed prettier all of a sudden in her short, transparent evening dress; for the first time I saw her just as a woman, dazzling in her femininity, at once unapproachable and aloof. Everything that I had found out about her over the course of the day, everything that had brought her closer to me—her alert, mischievous, lucid mind, her affectedly chummy directness, that sense of modesty that did not upset my own and that placed us both on an equal footing—all this, taken at face value (like a good mood or an unexpectedly agreeable book), was suddenly forgotten; it faded and receded, while Lyolya, unrecognizable in all her gay finery, was no longer mine but now living another life, one that was convivial, luxurious, and exclusive, provoking in me only a miserable sense of helplessness. Filled somehow with mortifying admiration, I saw her anew, and anew her hands, which only recently had seemed so nimble, domestic, and placid, but were now denudedly cold, hostile, and hence attractive; her soft, strong shoulders, her legs, became unattainable—never before had I scrutinized their impeccable feminine elegance. Another discovery: Lyolya is not at all the delicate thing that I imagined her to be in my initial affectations; rather, she is fine-boned, gracefully sculpted, with dainty little ankles and wrists, and perhaps it is from this that her apparent, deceptive frailty derives. Her most remarkable asset is her skin—of such tender and delicate whiteness, it exudes warmth and fading sweetness.

Lyolya—it strikes me for the first time that it would be more correct to write "Yelena Vladimirovna," as I am embarrassingly obliged to call her to her face—clocked how taken aback I was, and was manifestly pleased with the impression she had made, but she immediately took pity on me and tried to remedy the situation by drawing me into a series of mundane discussions imbued with playful candor, which has already become a habit of ours and, apparently, a refuge in moments of danger:

"I'm afraid my dress isn't fashionable enough—it's obvious I'm just a girl from the provinces. But we can't have you feeling ashamed of me—if everything comes off nicely, we'll see to the needs of my wardrobe together."

Gradually—because of this sweet, soothing tone, because of the opera cloak covering her bare arms and shoulders, because of the darkness in the taxi—I regained my former carefree, jaunty confidence, and only in the restaurant, when as if by chance I would find Lyolya beside me ("finding" a companion is a recurrent feature of my erratic nature) or detect somebody else's shameless, stubborn scrutiny—only then would I somehow shudder inwardly and for a moment lose sight of what I had found in Lyolya and taken from her—a dependable sense of equilibrium and support. And so it was that, like this, without that acute, wrenching anxiety, but calmly and cheerfully (quite unlike yesterday), I listened to the music, unmoved by its maudlin lyrics with their artificial relevance, and drank in moderation—owing both to a lack of necessity and to the possibility that Lyolya might have objected to my inebriation: she enjoys a certain mental well-being, one that she imparts to me—one that is, moreover, not crude, but lively and intelligent. Lyolya seemed to divine my thoughts and, as it were, wished to prove to herself that she was not deceiving me. After a lull in conversation, apropos of nothing, she blurted out:

"People think I'm sensible, unflappable, hard-nosed, that everything's been plain sailing for me. But it hasn't always been that way—true enough, I defied adversity where I could. I'll muster my strength tomorrow and tell you all about it."

I, too, wanted to come across as the sort of man Lyolya favored—healthy, successful, powerful: without resorting to falsehood, I gleaned, renewed even, this potential of mine (one of many) and called to mind rare instances of my indisputable success, perilous adventures, deeds, women who had surrendered themselves to me for a few brief moments; I exaggerated, added touches of color here and there, and it all came out as though my own aspirations were of little conse-quence to me—how easily I surrender them and how wearily I contemplate them. As Lyolya heard me out approvingly, however—she has a touchingly conscientious manner of listening—she suddenly remarked, after an argument about modern music:

"All the same, you like Tchaikovsky and Chopin—you're a dreamer."

I was hurt, as though I had been caught in some absurd, juvenile act, but in that moment (as always) all that counted was our friendship, which permitted such conversations; a new confidence—that at last I was "fixed up," taken, captured almost, that I no longer had to look for anything—filled me, imparting a sense of warmth and gratitude, driving out everything else. My dance partner from the previous night was sitting opposite me with a vague, contemptuous smile on her lips, and she was altered almost to the point of unrecognizability, independently of my present comfortable state, and seemed even outwardly—in comparison with Lyolya's radiant kindness—wooden and severe.

En route home, as soon as we found ourselves in a taxi, something again changed inside me (an aftereffect of the Gypsy music and the wine, brought on by our unintentional seclusion): once more I found myself looking at the Lyolya that I had discovered late that afternoon—seminaked, dazzling in front of the mirror—and, without a word of explanation, I began to kiss her hands (which until then had been so singularly alluring and out of reach, unforgettable for even a moment), but I did not kiss them boorishly, as I might have wanted, but with that usual disingenuous tenderness that every one of us can muster if only we ape infatuation, which was necessary here, lest I repulse and offend Lyolya. I was clumsy—I know this to be true—but Lyolya seemed touched, commending me amicably and freeing herself:

"Thank you, my dear, for the evening—you engineered it all admirably. Till tomorrow, then."

Now this "tomorrow" has dawned, one of those maddening days that are spoiled from the very outset, when, having awoken, you do not know what went wrong the previous evening, when you look for something to find fault with and then recall some heated, unnecessary words, a careless act that will seem frivolous, deceitful, irrevocably binding, and this sense of having made an irrevocable mistake now permeates everything, irrespective of what might happen before sleep comes again, and there remains (because of the impossibility of undoing what has been done or taking back what has been said) a single desire—to hide, to sleep, and never to wake up. What annoys me about yesterday, what humiliates and haunts me, is the way I kissed Lyolya's hands in the taxi (this is not merely regret for my clumsy, untimely impulse, but the perhaps exaggerated memory of Lyolya's having been touched too much)—this ghastly letdown has somehow erased yesterday's joy, a squandered joy, much too quickly over, and our new friendship appears to be one of wearisome, unbearable limitation. As I begin to reflect on this, I find that I am back in exactly the same boring, barren position in which I found myself before Lyolya's arrival (or, rather, before the arrival of Katerina Viktorovna's letter), that I am returning to my perennial, never-changing rut, that

Lyolya's chance appearance was an aberration ("desperation or fabrication"), and that the time has come for me to lock myself away, to leave—but suddenly I am fearful: for Lyolya is rightly waiting for something, and it is hard, impossible even, for me to ice over again, so it dawns on me that I have the option to fight, that we ourselves choose much of what constitutes our fate, the basis and tenor of diverse relations, we push ourselves amid uncertainty and often do this half-consciously or by complete accident, and so now the time has come for me to choose, but there is only one choice: Lyolya. Yet I must somehow explain away my current disillusionment—let the morning (half-asleep, unaccountable, disappointing as ever) take the blame—and so, without having allowed myself to come to my senses, and fearing new doubts and an irrevocable leap backward to my old, comfortable, attractively sedate life, I hurry now to Lyolya ahead of the agreed time.

December 14

FROM THE FIRST glance, from those very first words, it once again felt easy and endlessly diverting to be with Lyolya, and I did not have to force myself to make the slightest bit of effort. We spent the whole day together; I accompanied her on her various errands and, if ever I found myself alone in a café or in the street, I would feel somehow forlorn and would reckon the minutes, my mind blank—on occasion those necessary but dull entr'actes that break up a captivating theater piece are similarly desolate: so we try not to guess, not to expect, not to work ourselves up over what is to come. There is something that is forever joyous about my conversations and my relationship with Lyolya—I find it difficult to break free of my own accord, to go away even for a short while, I connive with myself to find ways of deferring obligatory meetings that take me away from her, and with a sense of tedium I submit to her troubles and cares alone. This can reach the point of absurdity: I myself proposed to speak to my debonair old boy about her (to fix her up as a designer in a fashion house) and, after she had readily agreed, I envisaged at once the dreary, solitary journey there and, lo, having invented some excuse, I pusillanimously deferred it.

I found my conversation with Lyolya today particularly absorbing—she had promised to tell me about herself the previous evening, and so I took her at her word and had eagerly anticipated her "confession" with an interest that was partly mercenary (as at the circus—she was to go through the fire, while I watched on and listened in safety) and partly apprehensive (what if her words were to move me!). I was uncertain how to remind her of what she had promised, but she herself—seemingly apropos of nothing—launched into it:

"I can just imagine how Auntie will have waxed lyrical about me and how she'll have tried to win you over. She told me there was no one able to listen and understand a person better than you, and that only you don't go in for winks and insinuations afterward. That sort of dependable understanding is just what I need, I haven't known it for the longest time—so here I am, ready to unburden myself to you."

This was not a preamble, nor was there any related "confession" to speak of, as I had so naïvely hoped there would be, but many times throughout the ensuing conversation we returned to Lyolya's past, and when I pressed her on various incidents and associations (without letting slip anything that Katerina Viktorovna had told me), she would answer me earnestly and in detail—indeed, she was trusting in all regards and audaciously candid.

I had already heard several times about Lyolya's first fiancé—about his work as an actor and what had become of him—but long ago I had begun to suspect that Katerina Viktorovna was holding back a great deal. These days he is a Moscow celebrity, widely held to be intelligent, cultured, and somehow more than his profession, which is rare among actors. At the same time, I have heard mentioned on more than one occasion—I even read about it in someone's memoirs—his dark, severe nature, his tyrannical neurosis, his fractiousness and unpleasant antics. I have—because of Lyolya and because of everything Katerina Viktorovna has told me—a long-standing rivalry-cum-infatuation with him: I absorb every little detail I can find out about him; his name in the newspapers is like that of a blood relative or a favorite poet, or like a mention of Russia in some foreign book. Today, it was a pleasure to reveal everything I had heard about him to

Lyolya—to show off my memory and carefully exhibit how much we had in common. I shall attempt to combine the fragmentary "confession" that Lyolya made in reply, to put it in order and relate it as accurately as possible:

"We were together for five years, during which we were hardly ever apart. When he was about to graduate from university, he was already preparing for the theater and was singularly, super-pedantically conscientious. That said, from the very outset he had an idea that we had to be on a par with one another, that he mustn't outshine me, and so, instead of springtime strolls, declarations of love, and going out on the town, we studied together diligently; he demanded my thoroughgoing participation in everything, forced me to overthink, and was awfully rude to me if I was ever lazy or unengaged. We immediately became very close—and it lasted five years. It will seem strange and objectionable to you: do try to understand, he shut out the world, keeping only me for company—I was awfully devoted to him, I didn't know how to repay him, and nothing I did ever seemed good enough. What's more, I bookishly thought that without 'it' there would be no trust in the relationship, no simple candor with one another, that before 'it' happens one person secretly strives for it, while the other balks at it, and both play games. I don't know why we never married—he directed the relationship unilaterally and seemed to be testing me or waiting for something. I thought that we had achieved such spiritual heights, where all extraneous matters—money, marriage, safeguarding the future—had become secondary and insignificant. During the last year of the war, he went off to his estate for a little while; when he came back, he suddenly announced that he didn't love me. I hadn't noticed his feelings cool prior to this, and he didn't seem to be besotted with anyone else after me. All my friends—Katerina Viktorovna included—were stunned and hazarded various explanations—she must have told you about this—but I didn't understand a thing. Perhaps my purpose had been to support him through those years while he was studying—though he believed in himself, he was ultimately alone and unadventurous. So, once he had begun to ingratiate himself with those theater types, he no longer needed me. Or maybe the reason was more ordinary: everything comes to an end, and my time was over. Ever since then I've had an incredible fear of inconsistency—as if anything could be taken from any one of us, and no power on earth would be capable of returning it. Still, he seems like a childish ideal that's out of reach, a clever dream, and quite from another world (compared to my more recent milieu)—he's a friend of commissars, an upstart, a Bolshevik."

I listened to Lyolya with a sorrow that was jealous but lacking malice and easily reconcilable: Sergei N. had enjoyed everything for which I did not even dare to hope, everything I held to be rightful but beyond my reach, everything manly and proper: five miraculous years with a Lyolya who was younger than her present self and hopelessly devoted to him; his diligent hard work in private, which had come off so well; his great success, which somehow always seemed justified and indicative of something—and yet, rapt, jealous, and sorrow-stricken, I unwittingly succumbed to Lyolya's feeling of his remoteness and otherworldliness, as if we were talking of an exciting new novel, and not of a life with which I had inadvertently come into contact, and which would forever be known to me.

After the death of her father (during the first months of Bolshevik rule), Lyolya went to live with Yekaterina Viktorovna in the south, and there, at the latter's insistence ("You can't be alone at a time like this"), she married a staff officer, a man of outward respectability, but far too wily and circumspect, the sort of man that was ten a penny back then—every one of them an impostor who, standing in the limelight and risking almost nothing, accepted the admiration and gratitude that was intended for other, undistinguished men, and who somehow magnanimously reflected their brilliance, daring, and merits. All of this, as well as her vain concern for her husband, who was consumed with the settling of scores and the politics of a world that was alien to her, Lyolya managed to discern only much later—during those terrible years she remained by his side, believed more than anyone in his spurious heroism and brilliance, and suffered the torments of the day's events and misfortunes. But there was something else that Lyolya was not telling me, something at which she only hinted, something that I divined (as I do everything

I find insulting or distressing) with pinpoint accuracy and precision—a hidden intent, the secret, sordid foundation of their relationship, something dangerous and insatiable inside Lyolya, and her husband's smug, triumphant power over her. I always greet such revelations with fear and trepidation; never do they tally with the grace and refinement of the calm woman I see before me, the woman who is outwardly so beyond sordidness and this freakish psychic blindness, and Lyolya reveals this in her own idiosyncratic manner—ashamedly, as if being drawn in again and shuddering because of everything that has come alive in her imagination—and a strange, dark, loathsome happiness bears down on me. My fear grows: the past is not yet gone and may still return, and in my memory yesterday's Lyolya appears again, like a bolt from the blue, sitting in front of the mirror, as does my bewildered, vaguely foreboding, and suddenly awakened sense of despair. But then a barely noticeable change transpires in her, she gets a handle on what she herself likely considers her dark and demonstrably immoral side, her rational calm seeks my own, joyously re-establishes the momentarily lost connection, and we find ourselves moving together again, curious friends anew, only now bearing a slight crack, the first in a future series of many, which is equally inevitable in both romantic and platonic relationships.

With self-deprecating perspicacity Lyolya raked over her distant and shameful memories—how she refused to allow, even banished the very notion of her fall, how she tried not to compare Sergei and her husband, how in the end, in Belgrade, in a difficult and exposing situation, she awoke to find beside her—she who was spent and yet still sober—an aging fool of a stranger, a man who was unbearable in his rash pursuit of prosperity, in his unthinking, unpalatable readiness to conform. Now the mistrust that had been so scrupulously hidden away grew wholly uninhibited and came out into the open, where it grew wild, and Lyolya, looking back and comparing, realized just how much fiction she had attributed to her husband, how low she had sunk and how it was high time and necessary for her to rise out of it. Here, she pronounced a verdict that astonished me—that to come down in the world did not mean losing one's former stature, that nothing is ever really lost, but that it is merely the attitude (to the stature) that changes, and that this attitude can be easily restored, and so there, in Belgrade, Lyolya attempted to restore her former attitude (and thus her former stature); she felt drawn to Berlin, and it was then that Katerina Viktorovna received a letter from her with a request for a visa, a request that was itself the genesis of our conversations about Lyolya, who then, having received the visa, and without waiting for a divorce, left—only, she was too late to catch me in Berlin.

"Do you know what's so odd about it? My husband—insignificant and deposed though he may be—still exists somewhere, he's not a dream like Sergei. That isn't because he came after, though; there's another reason, one you probably know yourself: everything on our side of the Russian border seems somehow closer, more tangible, whereas it's as if what's on the other side has been taken away from us forever."

I have long shared Lyolya's sense of Russo-Soviet other-worldliness, but the words that her husband is closer to her pricked me, as though I were not entirely free of some danger associated with him, and so today's new jealousy is concentrated on him alone, while for Sergei there remains only the dull reflection of an envy that is anemic and scarcely interesting.

In order to rank myself alongside the two of them, I imagined (quite artificially) that Lyolya's different paths had combined in me—from Sergei, his uplifting and worthy influence; from her husband, victorious strength (if I can overcome my initial shyness)—the upshot being that Lyolya, discovering all this in me, would want for nothing else and settle down with me alone, but such a rationale was of course a sly and lifeless sophistication, one that excited me but momentarily. Taking my cue from Lyolya, I too fancied a spot of candor about myself, but after her it all sounded unconvincing (a fact I had marked from day one)—even my voice failed me, seeming quiet and wooden, and, as always, the smooth coherence of my tales was confounded, arrested by what is commonly called gentlemanliness, by the fact that it has become an inane shibboleth in the context of today's changed views and the mores of many women to boast, to reveal one's relationships, by the rules I nevertheless obey, owing to age-old habit and the fear of violating some hard-won (though quite fallacious) sense of irreproachability, much as those who are renowned as experts continue to read tedious, pointless books—not only for the sake of their estimation in the eyes of others, but also to maintain their immaculate sense of probity before themselves.

Perhaps my reciprocal candor was not strictly necessary after Lyolya's confession: thanks to her, a common atmosphere has built up around us, we have things to argue about, things that raise a conspiratorial smile, our own familiar, allusive turns of phrase and, for every new occasion, words of caution drawn from experiences known to us both, that sense of complicity and seclusion (amid all others, who are alien to us and uninitiated), without which true friendship cannot exist. There was a time when I would covet this gift of an easy—almost inspired—foundation to a relationship and believe that it was secured by romantic success, by all sorts of prosperity in life; I believed also that I had been denied this gift, that I needed someone else's benevolent assistance, an initial jolt from some outside force, and so now, with gratitude, I rejoice that Lyolya is both willing and able to afford me this assistance.

December 15

TODAY IT WAS my turn to assist Lyolya, to repay her—in truth, my good offices are superficial, they are easier to give and cost less than our spiritual rapprochement, which

Lyolya has established imperceptibly and which continues to astound me, as does any successful attempt to draw together, to find or solve something in the mystery of human relations, in those impenetrable psychic depths: so often it seems to me that nothing could be more difficult, more vital, more challenging, and no matter how advantageous or beneficial someone else's exceptionally rare success may be, I cannot bring myself to trust its would-be significance.

That is why, when faced with so many celebrated and illustrious people, I am always captivated and touched by the same types, those few artists, thinkers, and doctors who have found their own, almost ineffable clarity with regard to those mysterious and labyrinthine psychic laws and have not feared the idle scorn of their contemporaries: to me it seems that these individuals (and others, too, whose risible sobriquet—"genius without portfolio"—is common enough, though cold comfort to me), that they alone need that unhappy, restless, forever-searching internal motion that we call a "divine spark," "creative faculty," and which likely connects only businessmen, politicians, and military commanders, as it becomes ensnared in the austere weight of their comparatively light ambition—to woo the crowd (always the same one), or else to perform machine tasks, tricks of chess and mathematics.

It fell to me to establish Lyolya, to set her up with work, but from long experience I hesitated to make any commitments, lest I be dashed against a rejection, lose heart at the first setback, squander my strength in a flurry of vain activity, and so I set out to see my old boy with something else in mind entirely: still, somewhere inside me—because of my compulsion to help Lyolya and thanks to the absence of any pressing deadline (they are always so brittle and meaningless)—there remained a lingering certainty that I would patiently, without disturbing that most vulnerable part of myself, keep returning, again and again, to this same point until I achieved my end. What is more, I had made no promises, lest I accept Lyolya's thanks (as yet unmerited and hence binding and shameful), lest I later dread embarrassed acknowledgments and her (even hidden) chagrin, and for yet another reason, too, one that is probably familiar to many: the less important what we try to achieve for ourselves (I am talking of those lazy and fainthearted souls like myself), the stronger and more assured we are, and often for the sake of success we must deceive ourselves and suppress what is necessary and essential to us—in any case, we are guaranteed (since it is "necessary and essential," all the same) to return to it despite ourselves. And so it was today: deliberately without laying the groundwork, avoiding the exhausting ambiguousness of preambles, still preoccupied with my own affairs, I launched into a conversation with Monsieur Derval regarding the purpose of my visit and showed him some of Lyolya's Berlin work. He was, as he always is with me, indulgent, in a fatherly sort of way; he accepted the drawings and bore them off to an adjoining room to consult somebody (this was the only moment when

I experienced any sense of exhilaration—at the prospect of my success or failure), before returning with a smile:

"*C'est épatant.* Is your friend young? Of course we'll take her." (My old boy is involved in no less than ten ventures of the most diverse nature.) "Bring her here tomorrow and we'll discuss the terms. Or better yet, let's the three of us have dinner at mine this evening." (Monsieur Derval is a bachelor.) "I've been meaning to invite you for so long."

I could have gone to Lyolya triumphant, but to flaunt one's triumph, even in the most sincere and well-meaning way, is never advantageous: altruistic help, like friendship, love, business, and all sorts of other alliances, requires guile, calculation, an agenda—with naïvely blustering, brutish ingenuousness, we pique our ally's proud and natural human dignity, some sense of rivalry that is always at hand, and we risk turning a strong alliance into a competition. I trained myself long ago to see a particular charm in postponing my triumphs, and I could not believe it when just the other day Lyolya (apropos of the discreet financial assistance that I had given Katerina Viktorovna) unexpectedly put me to shame. Today, however, Lyolya was only too pleased—sans calculation, sans agenda—to show her gratitude, and this was a perfectly faithful sign of her disposition to me: after all, we do not like being indebted to people who are indifferent or unpleasant. She scarcely mentioned the evening, our dinner with Monsieur Derval, but for all the confidence she displayed in front of me, for all her level-headed composure, she was nervous and had studiously prepared, as if fearing that this cosseted old Parisian might not take to her, or, rather, as though having decided that he jolly well would take to her and that, in so doing, she would delight me and prove herself in some way. Perhaps I am mistaken and have ascribed to Lyolya my own childish hope—to rise up through the help of Monsieur Derval—but so often, during the course of our various conversations, it has been painfully obvious to me that we are both of us thinking the same thing, and it seems that Lyolya has realized this, too.

The sweet old boy made good on his promise, lavished praise on Lyolya's designs, her taste and manner of dressing, on my probity and business acumen, and at length tried to persuade Lyolya to use her influence on me ("You really will make short work of him"), lest I idle or neglect deals that have already met with initial success, and he whispered delightedly to me, as though astonished even by his own delight (the French are truly adept at endearing themselves with amusing allusions to all manner of romantic circumstances): *"Mais elle est charmante, votre amie, et bien tranquille."* This final point was true: indeed we had come *en famille*, as some provincial couple, all trusting smiles, and this kindly, hospitable atmosphere, this unhurried, modest repast, this benevolent, solicitous patronage corresponded to our peaceable relations (which consisted mostly in a lethargy that was blissfully restful), just as drunken revels, squandering money, and an admiration for suicide correspond to the first symptoms of loutish desperation, while the forest or the sea and a bench by the beach correspond to a fresh new feeling, one that is oblivious to the fact that it might still end badly.

Lyolya seemed perhaps even too calm; I was amazed that she was able—without rushing, easily and intelligently—to keep the conversation with Monsieur Derval going, that she had no impatient desire to leave with me, no yearning for us to be alone together, all the sooner to share the impressions that I had been accruing for her and that had not yet found a way out. It seemed vital that I should remind her not only of the flattering remarks made to each of us, but also of Monsieur Derval's amusing words, our successful rejoinders, and, judging by what had been said, the opportunities awaiting us; moreover, I was keen to show off my powers of memory and observation and jubilantly ascertain just how closely our individual observations coincided. But Lyolya was in no rush, and I fear that such patience as she has (which may well be common to all women) is a great advantage over me: this may be the initial reason that I am drawn to her more strongly than she is to me. When the dinner was over, however, and we found ourselves—after coffee and liqueurs—alone in the street, she was no less delighted than I: in step and arm in arm, like a regular couple that has come to an arrangement long ago, we set off along the endless embankments, amicably and amiably discussing the details of our agreeable visit, and I was astonished how psychologically stronger I felt as a result of this sweet and loyal support and how quickly I have become habituated to my newfound cossetedness, which habit I cannot shake.

December 21

A STRANGE TRANSFORMATION is taking place—or, dare I even say, has taken place—within me, one that has been caused, of course, by Lyolya, and that is telling on my attitude toward her, on our conversations, and all sorts of other things. Lyolya has been working for several days now and has made me promise not to bother her at work; we meet in the evenings, dine together, but in the daytime I am almost always alone. During the hours when she is employed and, according to the terms of our "arrangement," inaccessible, I dreamily and patiently await the arrival of evening, and only on rare occasions, forgetting myself, indulging myself, do I suddenly recall, with a palpable sense of certitude, that we live in the same city, that all it would take for me to hear her kind, soothing voice is one telephone call or a ride on the Métro—and right now I feel the need for this, as for consolation in a time of despair. Never yet have I succumbed to this tempting desire; I do not cast about for casual pretexts, however plausible they may be, and so, owing to such (purely outward) control, owing to my ensuing spiritual dissatisfaction, my impatience becomes keener and all the more exigent, and our evening rendezvous, which are much too friendly and sensible, do not always assuage me.

Still more astonishing is my newfound attitude toward other women: many of them—as it so happens, even the young and attractive ones—irritate me now; wistfully I endure the usual polite conversation, which seems intent on reminding me that it is not Lyolya who now sits before me, that it is she, her aura, that I need, that she is the one thing to which I am accustomed, and that any other woman's charms merely tease me with some semblance, a hint at similitude, or otherwise seem hopelessly, blandly foreign. This is one manifestation of love's cruel injustice, which I have long known (only, the shoe is most often on the other foot, and I the victim) and which never deceives.

Perhaps I should not have even noticed these transformations, had I not been left so out of sorts by my acute exhaustion after today's excitement. Lyolya had planned to spend the evening with distant relatives and agreed to meet me later at the bistro opposite her hotel. Several times I asked her—half-jokingly but still humiliatingly—not to be late, and she airily promised to be there no later than eleven o'clock. Having made up my mind that she would be sure to turn up at the appointed hour, and that perhaps by some miracle she might even appear a little earlier, I ensconced myself in that stifling, cramped little bistro immediately after dinner, with a volume of poetry and my old notebooks, which every once in a while (so that each time my former impression has had sufficient time to fade) I lovingly read over, but neither the verses nor my naïve, half-forgotten conjectures about individuals and their emotions touched me, as if—burnt already by an incipient, vague sense of unease, by a fever that was still objectless and auguring something yet to come—I myself had grown drearier than these very combinations of names and words, which had moved me so recently but now seemed little more than a vapidly flickering inventory. When I realized that they would bring me no succor, that I should have to face up to my nascent impatience, which was fated to grow yet, to drain and torment me for a further hour and a half—an incalculable number of moments, like those that had just gone before them and every bit as unbearable—I simply surrendered myself to hopeless, destructive, limp impatience, unashamed of my morbid weakness and, in a sense, childishly gloating that now, because of Lyolya, because of her negligence and disregard, our sweet and friendly evening ritual is ruined, and I am perforce obliged to suffer the torments of this opaque, hostile atmosphere, in which I am being slowly and imperceptibly poisoned—by cup after cup of hateful, bitter coffee mixed with some kind of grounds, by the air, leaden with bodies and smoke and reeking of poverty, by my immediate wicked and vindictive suspicions that have unwittingly been provoked . . .

But now all this is over, that long hour and a half has passed; for some reason, it has lodged itself in my memory divided into different parts, each distinct from the other, each connected with different people around me, with different ratios of hope and bitterness, with different degrees of impatience (thus we sometimes divide a summer spent in various places into disparate, perfectly isolated segments), and at last I feel better: after all, Lyolya may yet come; I ought to keep my eye on the opening door, hope to see her beige glove on the door handle and then her telltale elegant silhouette and gay, narrowed eyes.

Suddenly, a perfectly admissible, simple hypothesis suggested itself to me: what if twenty minutes were to pass, then half an hour, then an hour, and Lyolya still did not show up, and I, none the wiser, was obliged to return home—how should I bear this, how should I cope with the obtrusive nocturnal visions that would then be so warranted and natural, how could I wait to see them disproved? I recollected once again the dark, forbidding side of Lyolya—something to which I had not given sufficient consideration, lulled by these recent calm days, and all of a sudden I seemed to wake up, forced to admit to myself that this was precisely what had so captivated and beguiled me about her in the first place, and so my nascent culpability was revealed to be equally dark and forbidding.

But there was more—inexplicable though quite credible forebodings of some rivalry, conflict, someone else's victory and (after many ordeals) my own dubious, ostensibly fortunate repose. The more time passed, the more likely this possibility became—of rivalry or someone else's victory—and there seemed to be no other plausible explanation for

Lyolya's lengthy absence. In effect, two opposing states had traded places within me—an agency, when I had been ready to accept Lyolya's dangerous witchcraft, to cope with it some-how, to combat it, when her cruel absence bore one (decidedly ugly) explanation, one to which I could not be reconciled and which never ceased to torment me—and another, simpler, state, one of passive amenity and weakness. In these helpless moments, I seemed to content myself with Lyolya's friend-ship, tried not to see what was dangerous and alarming about her, tried to convince myself that even now nothing decisive would happen, that after such mutual goodwill, after all our revelations of the wrongs we had suffered and our fear of committing those wrongs against another, after today's humiliating request, Lyolya could not "betray" me, dis-appear, fail to turn up, and so I recovered my initial faith in her smiling, cheerful materialization, which would restore the past, and ascribed her late arrival to those silly accidents that I, too, so often encounter, to the fact that it is always I who organize meetings with friends and acquaintances, I who invite them, remind them, wait for them, as though the burden of establishing friendly or cordial relations rests solely on me, I who must guide and maintain them, while the only cause of all these hurtful misunderstandings is in fact my excessive scrupulousness.

Strange though it may seem, it was not my strength but my weakness that proved the more astute: around one o'clock in the morning, when the chairs in the bistro were being cleared away and I, jaded by the monotony, had given up all hope but not quite resolved to leave, the beige glove that had so stubbornly absented itself made its appearance from behind the door, followed by Lyolya, wearing a smile of disguised embarrassment that was only too ready to erupt at my very least complaint. But even now there were no feelings of indignation, nor could there be any: what I had gone through in those few hours—impatient expectation, the fear of loss, the prospect of a long, unbearable, feverish night—had miraculously dissipated, vanished with Lyolya's appearance, to be reborn some other day, provoking my real, no longer fictitious jealousy, and then, after years—perhaps after our rupture and my newfound tranquility—suddenly to emerge again in a perverse, oppressive, pitifully contrived anamnesis, of the kind that had enlivened my abject loneliness only recently. I was amazed and even alarmed by this sudden discovery of Lyolya's sway over me—it had been so easy and required no effort on her part to mortify the desperation that she had provoked: not only did I find myself irrevocably at her mercy, but I simply had nowhere to hide—my former oneiric anticipation of her had been replaced by her living presence, dislodged by it, dead forever, and now Lyolya's departure could precipitate such hopeless emptiness, of a kind I had never yet known. This hopelessness likely compelled me, without question or deliberation, to forgive Lyolya in an instant, and in all likelihood I should have consented to any, even the most shameful, act just to forestall her potential disappearance. Lyolya understood all this in her own way, and a victorious, patronizing smile flitted across her face, only to be quelled instantly, and now she addressed me no longer as an equal, but as though offering me a gift that I had to accept with gratitude and humility:

"I'm glad I caught you—I was being held prisoner by the dullest people. I shan't be paying them another visit. It's cold here—why don't we slip up to my room and sit together for a little while? Don't forget, I have to be up early again tomorrow morning."

As I close my eyes, I try to envisage Lyolya, as I once imagined her, as she appeared to me at the railway station, but now she seems unrecognizably altered, like so many people about whom one's first impressions, when revived after a long friendship, seem inexplicably naïve and far removed. With Lyolya, when she was imaginary and hardly known to me, I had associated, for the most part, a calm sense of trust, a mutually gratifying tenderness (or, if nothing else, a constant readiness to experience it), those rare and extraordinary things that were all that remained of my previous love affairs in my psychic memory, eclipsing them and continually drawing me in, things that were now retreating, being replaced by a honeyed, rapacious hope—to steal Lyolya away from someone, to kidnap her and make her choose me—a hope forever mixed with the fear of failure and loss, a hope that essentially pervaded each of my prior emotions: only on rare occasions have I achieved that easygoing, magnanimous distance that is

preserved only in my psychic memory and which I errone-
ously ascribed to Lyolya and our imaginary relationship.

I do not know whether Lyolya's *noblesse* has truly waned
or whether it only seems that way, or whether she is playing
some inescapable, unwittingly cruel game, but even now,
calmed as I am by her, in a moment of cool-headed caution, as
I search for a means of giving despair the slip, just as I did
today, I do not strive to strike a friendly deal with Lyolya, but
rather I want (like a man who loves hesitantly) to be sure to
outwit her with my art, and it is just as hard now to divorce
myself from this new hope, from this new, ever-threatening
fear of mine (as I did only recently, from dreariness and boredom) as it is impossible to divorce oneself from inconsolable
grief or from that surfeit of well-being by which I am visited so
rarely and always to no avail. And yet, no matter how much
suffering yet awaits me, I shall be glad of Lyolya's cruel game;
most of all, I fear that she has taken it into her head not
to return me to my original loveless calm, which is so far
removed from the blissful peace of reciprocity, but—
inimically, hopelessly—to stay with me forever.

Today I am finding it difficult to write—for the first time
since I learned of Lyolya's impending arrival. Back then, at
the start of all this, I set about my excited preparations in
anticipation of her, only to be struck dumb by our unexpectedly amicable first encounter—from those new possibilities
proceeded a constant succession of observations, deductions,
well-placed and seemly words, which would accumulate

throughout the day and which I, fearing to muddle them, would rush to commit to paper in the evenings. After overcoming the initial tiresome and (for me) inescapable obstacles—the crumpled paper in my pocket, the pencil that is never sharp enough, the awareness that all this means many hours of isolation—I would be drawn into my work surreptitiously and often fail to notice how other fortuitous discoveries would be added to what I had struck upon and come up with earlier, how difficult it would be for me to exchange their original unwieldy obscurity for a clear and orderly sequence. Such effort—the need for sustained thought and observation—would by no means weaken, but rather intensify each of my impressions, imparting to them a distinct—drawn from a demonstrable reality—living, genuine meaning with a guaranteed duration, and so I had something with which to justify the work, to which all my time tended, and my only regrets would be the incompleteness of my writing, the bouts of inertia, fatigue, and sloth. But today my experience suggests something else—that it is no longer worth writing, thinking, observing, that I cannot twist the focus of my psyche, which is directed at one thing alone, by forcing and diverting it, that my scribblings themselves will come out just as I am now—feverishly monomaniacal—and that I shall experience, as I have always done, an interim period of calm when my current impetuous fever, while not letting up, will merely diminish (although all-consuming oblivion will never come), and then I shall try to restore everything that was omitted and slowly put everything in order, while in this condition—desperate, sickly, unable to be reasoned with—like a drunkard bereft of his senses, the cleverest thing for me to do would be to keep my peace.

And yet, there is something that still yearns to be expressed, for all that a time in my life (one that I have regarded as uniquely happy) is now at an end, and for all that my scribblings about it are ending, too; perhaps it is my attitude to this time that remains unexpressed, or rather unestablished, and I do not know with which emotion—tenderness, bitterness, or boredom—I shall read over what I have written during these strange days, nor do I know what I shall regret, what I shall want to recapture and revive, and what will seem disappointingly inessential. Such a retrospective, mature, definitive appraisal will depend on one thing alone—how matters turn out for Lyolya and me, how they end—for a good or bad ending will color it all, mar it in our memory, as sometimes the final words of a poem illuminate anew everything that went before them (but then, whatever our appraisal of love and those whom we have loved, what will stand out in our memory is the beauty of even a moment's reciprocity—that and our hope, forever alive, within reach, on the verge of coming true). I cannot clearly define what I mean by "a good end," but I do try to believe in at least a fleeting success with Lyolya, in spite of the many warning signs and the disappointments of my past that would persuade me otherwise, and I can in fact, without deception, prove to myself that my current choice is the only right one: never to this day have I met anyone who could match Lyolya's compassionate resolve in all things, anyone with her sense of responsibility toward me or who evinces the simple idea that I am indispensable, and never have I, with any woman but for Lyolya, been able to talk without that ghastly, deprecating other voice that appears the moment I catch a woman out and, for my own sake, expose her frailty or deceit and for coming from a different (base and shallow) life, the moment I perceive my own isolating and frankly loathsome superiority. By this I do not mean to boast—at times judgments that unconsciously appraise, unconsciously compare, emerge within us, and we conform to them, caring nothing for their accuracy, against all our generosity of spirit. But there is no such danger with Lyolya, seeing that she is incapable of the rebukes, the henpecking, the mindless hostility typical of so many weak and absurd women, and if matters turn out unfavorably with her, then the blame will fall on me, or on the hand of fate, which seems to have set out to guide me—through torments and hindrances—toward a morbid insight, one that claims nothing for itself and favors no one, and so projects a sense of justness. This is not a pose, nor is it a chance invention of mine: I know what the reckoning will be.

PART II

I T HAS ALREADY been two weeks since Lyolya left Paris. With a speed that has surprised even me, I have managed to regain my composure, or, rather, I have liberated myself from that initial rebellious sense of despair, the one that did not understand life without Lyolya, without those festive, habitual, essential hours with her. The fever, the constant intoxication of these last months, has been replaced by some-thing different, not as keen (since I am not made to get ready or to wait every other moment), but nobler, like everything that is undemanding, not graspingly proprietorial, by some-thing that is now guaranteed. Because I cannot see Lyolya, because I cannot seek her out or expect to encounter her (which was very nearly a perpetual preoccupation of mine, and of which I am now, as it were, unburdened), I again feel the desire to set down of an evening everything that happens to me, and this is not only a desire to express myself, but also an attempt to save from oblivion another special time in my life, to salvage something for my future, for the man that I anticipate and envisage myself to be in the years to come— changed and having forgotten many things. Never before have I been drawn so credibly to this apparently useless endeavor, and never has it so manifestly constituted a distinct part of my life, a distinct and consistent aim, more distinctive than money, pleasure, or books, and second in terms of its appeal to one thing only: what Lyolya might have been—but there is no Lyolya, nor, it seems, will there be. My desire "to write" begins to resemble a passion, one that is attended by impatience and a hatred for people or things that stand in my way: I have surrounded myself with ridiculous obligations that seem as if by design to sap away every hour of the day and evening, and frequently (as at the mention of something tactless or particularly offensive) I avert my eyes when people invite me to stay or go off with them somewhere. And yet, still I found it difficult to overcome that inevitable first bit of inertia, and every time, as soon as I would find myself alone—in a café during the day or in my room late at night—I would write nothing and breezily absolve myself on grounds of noise, distractions, or fatigue. Even now, as I sit before these large, smooth sheets of paper, which are being filled thanks to my exertions, there still remains a neurasthenic fear of work, of doing harm unto myself, of the necessary will.

I saw off Lyolya with that utmost despair that emotionally well-brought-up people try not to show and that even in their recollections they only mention by name, because that sort of despair is shameless and strips a person wickedly—it is only too pleased to do anything absurd and lurid if it means announcing its presence and shouting at the top of its lungs—and later on it will seem a perfect miracle, one that has saved us from irrevocable humiliation, that we managed to hide all that or at least never once to say a word about it: we ourselves scarcely suspect how treacherously our appearance betrays us, how we must rejoice (and, more importantly, content ourselves) if no one can find fault with our careless actions or words. My despair at the time was caused by the fact that Lyolya—manifestly—was leaving me, and it grew larger on account of one specific feature inherent in so many goodbyes—the impression that the person doing the seeing-off is being abandoned. True, sometimes the seer-off will return to his usual rut, to his work or friends, while the person leaving will seem abandoned, alone among others in the carriage, but with Lyolya and I it happened the other way around (and thus not the exception, but the rule): I did not know where to turn without her, while she journeyed off to Berlin, at the request, at the summons of Sergei N. All throughout the despair—it was worse at the station than at any other time before then—I felt that it would soon pass, and indeed, with every day it did become easier to bear, until at last I reached that agreeably unhappy state, with its frequent sharp pricks and the constant fear of being pricked, a state that will likely prove robust and long-lasting: at any rate, I do not envisage or imagine its end or any possible substitution.

Why did calm come so quickly, and is there not something in it that debases my irrefutable feelings for Lyolya? In a shrewd and observant French novel I recently read: *"L'amour supporte mieux l'absence ou la mort, que la doute et la trahison."* This simulacrum of an explanation—that everything can be reduced to romantic egotism, which selects from various possibilities the most placid one for itself (relatively speaking)—this intimation seemed to open the floor to uneasy speculations, and I could but impotently and honestly admit to myself that I had no real words of my own, nor any explanation.

Perhaps another reason that I mastered myself so quickly was that right after Lyolya's departure a new affliction befell me—penury, and all the ghastly to-do and running about that goes with it: they say that one misfortune, when compounded by another, does not increase the acuity or strength of those painful, bitter feelings, but rather ought to diminish them and help us cope with them; more to the point, an idle, chance unpleasantness can sometimes devour a hefty concern, imperceptibly eating into it, cutting it down to size, to its easily borne negligibility, and vindicating, as it were, the proverb "fight fire with fire." I have often wanted—in moments of grief or fear—to cause myself deliberate physical pain (something like an inoculation from psychological pain), to attempt to recall something humiliating, shameful, unforgivable in my past: in this present suffering there is a pretentious inner posture that believes in its own righteousness and stands indignant before fate, and so it is necessary to deprive it of its nobility, its righteousness, its fervent belief in these things, to sweep out from under it the most solid foundation for any postures of suffering—a sense of injustice, a resentment of one's fate—and only then is deliverance possible. Granted, there will be an element of unwitting self-deceit to begin with: even before Lyolya's departure I looked indifferently, with a maniac's unconcern for everything extraneous, on the money that was slipping through my fingers and the little that remained, thinking dismally that soon enough some dreary worries, troubles, blandishments would burst in on my cruel abandonment, that I should have to conceal much about myself from Derval or anyone else, that it would be especially hard to master and bestir myself in the midst of despair, and I had not supposed just how this would evolve into an almost accidental distraction, how all this breakneck (never having time for pause), eternal business—not being late, meeting, waiting, searching for addresses, stairwells, interchanges in the Métro—would gradually take shape, and how on the heels of these affairs (which are uncontrived, obligatory, and have been rudely imposed on me) the inevitable joys of achievement or grievances of disappointment would appear, annihilating (temporarily, of course) all my foregoing pain—and when that pain rears its head again, it will seem superficial and more easily borne, no matter how new, how fresh and acute it may seem at the moment when it returns. There may well be a kind of suffering that is inconsolable and lingering, but Lyolya's departure, which did not graze my romantic egotism and has not proved fatal, has been upstaged, mollified by these initial distractions, among which penury is not the only one.

Another distraction has come in the form of the Wilczewski family. As with everything that surrounds and occupies me at the moment, the Wilczewskis appeared on the scene in Lyolya's final weeks, and even then our bland encounters had become a regular occurrence. In truth, I had always— since my Petersburg days—known them a little, and news of them reached me continually, but I had no personal relationship with them to speak of, and despite all my curiosity for even the remotest and most uninteresting of people, I do not believe that I ever once thought of them. I do not quite understand how it came about that Bobby Wilczewski one evening, amid the drunken clamor at a renowned haunt in Montparnasse, unexpectedly came up to Lyolya and me, smiling as though he had at last managed to find his friends; he sat down with us until late in the evening, and together we saw Lyolya home, who laughingly heard out his incessant anecdotes. Boring and monotonous though they were, Bobby's appearance and his idle talk enlivened our conversation, which had been strained, like all conversations at that affrontingly inexplicit hour, and I only pitied that I could not subsequently be rid of him and alone with Lyolya, who by now had brightened up and was uncharacteristically (as she used to be) sweet; I tried to elaborate this to her, but she, by accident or design, failed to understand. We agreed to meet Bobby on the following day, and, what was more, he promised to bring along his sister, who was "forever sniveling that she has no one to go out with," and so after that the four of us began to see one another almost every day.

The Wilczewskis, having been of dubious wealth back in Petersburg, hardly find themselves flush in Paris, although they consider it a point of honor to "compete," and so, for them, the expenses, contacts, and connections of others are things that have held their value, things with which they still care to trouble themselves. There are three of them—a father, a son, and a daughter—and, although they are often together, they remain individuated in my imagination. The old man is a quick, sharp, always unshaven little man, whose questions are disjointed, designed to elicit confusion and fascination, and not at all the other person's answer; when there are guests, he will burst into the drawing room for a minute, and then just as quickly dart out again, leaving in his wake a general feeling of exasperation, disjunction, and a lingering sense of awkwardness. When I visited him for the first time— just before Lyolya's departure—he bizarrely tore into me on account of his son: "How can you be friends with that ass, who let happiness slip through his fingers today?" He was alluding to some minor business matter, but it came out so abominably, and en route home Lyolya rebuked me at great length—with sudden, unwarranted irascibility—for not having tried hard enough to hide my disgust.

The young Wilczewskis are for some reason patronizingly if affectionately called, both to their face and in their absence, "little Bobby" and "little Zina," despite the fact that "little Zina" has been married, divorced, and is, so it would seem, twenty-eight years of age. These frivolous names, however, are justified and natural-sounding: there is something lost and adrift about brother and sister, something that forever evades definition and is unintentionally pathetic; above all else, both siblings worship glamor, the success of others, without envy and with a certain desire merely to mimic the glamor that is beyond their reach—of course, in some modest, vicarious way. With "little Zina" this desire is directed (impotently and in a surprisingly old-fashioned manner) at "art," at little-known actors and writers; with Bobby it is more emphatic and grasping—at money and commerce. He even holds me to be a successful businessman, "with contacts" (on account of Derval), and talks to me with a touch of deference, as though any advice I gave would never fail to be heeded. Bobby is of average height, with sleek and shiny dark hair, which he wears in a parting; he has brilliant dark-chestnut eyes, rosy cheeks (as though he has just stepped in from the cold), dimples, and that ostentatiously cheeky smile of his, one that is forever seeking approval and infects no one, recalling somehow a hand hanging in midair. He is quite ungainly, too—because of his square torso, because of his hands, which are much too big (they look swollen) with their wooden fingers and broad, round nails, because of his heavy, clumsy feet—yet he does try to project a sort of elegance and has contrived his own "style" (gaiters, a motley though tolerable array of shirts and ties, a mincing gait), and next to Lyolya—as though in tune with her, although following no particular pattern—he would on occasion seem radiantly flamboyant and picturesque. Zina, on the other hand, is quite dull; she has an ashen face, the colorless hair of a darkling blonde, and also big, albeit pleasingly so, hands and, thanks to her low heels, a wide, graceless, almost masculine gait. What is striking, incongruous even, about her is her full, readily amenable, somehow shameless lips and her long, shapely (of the robust sort) legs, which she—without abashment or invitation—attempts to show off. Brother and sister, both tall and young, do not constitute, as one might expect, a balanced and neat couple: the confusion, the approximation that is so apparent in each of them requires—even for an outward comparison—some sound, additional support.

I should prefer to race through all these tedious descriptions, which are unnecessary in a work like this—one that is for myself alone—yet I cannot escape the persistent vain hope that one day these notes of mine (despite myself and, as it were, as a reward for my pains) will be read carefully by somebody, and so now, ahead of time, like a dewy-eyed child, I choose to believe in that reader, one who is understanding and kind, and shall wait until at last "she" (Lyolya, or else her successor and final incarnation) is found; then, we shall both deserve the miracle of mutual trust, and for "her," who will not know my former life, I shall prepare everything in good conscience, as futile and gratuitous as it may seem. Speaking for myself, superficial people, circumstances, "mass" events are nothing but vulgarity, a substitute for that real human essence that is so clearly involved in every single feeling, in every love, be it distressing or joyous, because our own uninhibited feelings and our careful, skilled reflection on them, frees us of the psychological dust that ordinarily covers everything, and it is a pity to waste on this, on superficial things, our brief, singular life that forever strives for flight but finds itself so heavily weighed down. "Real human essence"— these are not nonce words: in jealousy (be it one's own or observed in others), in every relationship that touches us, especially in romantic ones, there is, alongside what goes on and is experienced (even that which is suicidally tragic), some newborn novelty that revels in itself and is ravishingly alive, and for the sake of which it is giddyingly easy both to torment oneself and to die, something that is absent and not to be found in the respectability of the Wilczewski household, in Bobby's gaiters, in everything and everywhere from which it has been banished by superficial, wretchedly devised, deadening repetitions. I could yet vastly extend the scope of what is alive and what is dead, but I want to and must limit myself, otherwise a danger worse than living death will rear its head—that of preoccupation with chance, absence of will and dissipation.

Let me return to the Wilczewskis, if only for a brief moment: it pains me especially to write about them—for it is they who are the principal, absurd, unnecessary impediment to the simple and unattainable things that I seek all day long:

seclusion and the diarist's work. It used to seem to me as though Lyolya, in an attempt to avoid being left alone with me, to evade my reproaches and possibly too explicit interrogations, was consciously ensnaring me in the first group that presented itself; yet even in her absence the outcome would have been the same, and this is explained partly by my feeble lack of will and partly by my being overindulged—over the months with Lyolya I had gradually grown accustomed to people, begun fearing loneliness, and was ready to exchange it for anything that came my way, be it tedious or unseemly. Today at the Wilczewskis' I pondered this peculiar unscrupulousness of mine for the very first time—as always, the thought was provoked by something trivial and haphazard: as Zina was bidding farewell to someone, she said jokingly, "Do come again, now that you know how to find us" (she says this without fail to every new guest), and I unwittingly compared her to Lyolya, who could never trot out the same old smug commonplaces; it was not only Lyolya's absence and substitution by the Wilczewski lot, but also my whole day, its sense of being preordained, its artificiality, the rehearsedness of every minute, the never-ending haste—from the moment I open my eyes until that when I close them again—it all seemed unbearable to me, and now Zina's silly phrase, which inadvertently reminded me that nowhere around, among the others, is support or favor to be found, proved for me so significant that it has apparently forced me to take up once again my interrupted, isolating chronicle. All the same, I do need the Wilczewskis: they are, for the time being, my sole reminder of Lyolya, and just after her departure, they were as vital to me as blood—a consequence of the instantaneous psychological transition, so usual in such circumstances, from security, from the intoxication of someone else's presence, which we so especially cherish, to hopeless, cold abandonment, when those whom we have always held to be intrusive and superfluous suddenly become worthy, desirable companions; they ape something that has been lost, something precious and irreplaceable, and are able to touch us, to listen intelligently—and to surprise us with things still unknown.

Lyolya does not write about herself per se, and in two weeks I have received from her only a postcard sent en route—a sweet but dreadfully confused missive, which I have committed to memory, and which has long since become tattered in my trouser pocket. Not once since then have I had any news of her, and I know neither where she is nor what she is doing. I feel no initial resentment, and my relatively friendly letters (which I send to Katerina Viktorovna's Berlin address) neither reproach nor make demands.

June 18

M Y MOST TREASURED state of being, which I anticipate during business conversations and at the Wilczewskis', when I am busy or otherwise occupied, and to which I am ready to give myself over, singing, as soon as I find myself alone—in the street, in a café, in the Métro, or at home, in my room, before I fall asleep—I half-consciously want to dub, with words that are meaningless to others, "Lyolya and I." These words, pronounced almost inaudibly and with great relish, this sense of freedom—that everything is permitted and, consequently, I am permitted to think as I please about us both—these are what this state of being begins with, and it seems to continue my innumerable imaginary encounters with Lyolya, our unwritten, unsent letters, our hypothetical arguments that swell with indignation. All this began long ago, long before Lyolya's departure, when, after her first, petulant quibbling, after my timidity began to develop incrementally, the easygoing simplicity of even our outward friendship came to an end. Earlier still, before Lyolya, since time immemorial, if during the course of an evening I should forget to say something felicitous or crucial, then later, recalling this, I would not be able to sleep or find repose, and would compose phrases, find means by which to memorize them, sometimes—as though in a writer's fever—get up, switch on the light, and jot down something essential, and, I suppose, it was from these agitated nocturnal recollections of what had been forgotten, from this redressing of the past and what I had memorized, that this current, most pleasant state of being—one that is also a form of redress—was born.

Granted, what I wrote in those bygone years seemed second-rate even the morning after, but later, once Lyolya appeared on the scene, everything I prepared fell flat, since it was imposed artificially on a lively and unrelated conversation, and it is possible that now, too, during a real, non-imaginary encounter, all my contrived remarks would prove just as misplaced (how unlike my real letters are those that I imagine), but what so persistently and joyously engrosses me emerges and flows ever so naturally, seems so spot-on and right, as though it really were the natural, unencumbered development of my romantic relations, while the other, decent, reasonable path, the one that was never hidden from Lyolya, has simply been disfigured by her rebuff, and, in recent weeks, further still by her absence and distance.

The dynamism of my inner world, which is set in motion, as it were, by the magic words "Lyolya and I," is more loaded than I ever believed possible: rage, noble sentiment, tenderness—they all reach their limits without the slightest bit of reticence or restraint. At first I believed that someday I would give expression to everything amassed in me, and I tried to commit to memory at least what mattered (that because of Lyolya's proven treachery, for instance, I ought not to love her), but later—before long—that changed: practically since childhood I have been able to divide quite soberly what is real from what is imagined (and to move suddenly, almost imperceptibly, from one to the other), and so now, having realized the real vanity of my constant fictions about Lyolya, I have allowed myself to be charmed by them for their own sake, the very fact of which also entails a measure of self-preservation—it touches me without posing any danger.

I daresay such a game might have somehow influenced my current feelings for Lyolya, too, imbuing them with a mitigating artificiality, yet the fact itself that I divide what is real and what is imagined with almost unerring accuracy prevents their mutual interference, any penetration of one into the other.

Most often in my fantasies I enjoy rebuking Lyolya out of spite—I seem to have some kind of unending suit against her, owing to a multitude of offenses, and I find myself wanting not only to speak out, to tug at Lyolya's heartstrings, to try to win her back, but also to punish her, to convince her of the irreparability of her mistakes, the impossibility of my forgetting and returning to how things were, and so our relations permutate, as if Lyolya will come to me to make amends, and I cannot accept this. I have become so used to such a permutation, to my constant, sweet, justified spite, that I should find myself at a loss, were Lyolya in fact to come back to me, wanting to redress the past—but this will never happen.

I find innumerable faults in Lyolya (this current cruel absence of letters, her gross disregard for how easily I am hurt, her attempts to avoid explanations in the wake of her own words, which oblige her to be frank), but, even with all this in mind, I must own to my recent, bitterest discovery— that all this had in fact manifested itself (albeit pale and inert) long before Lyolya's departure, and even prior to Sergei N.'s decisive letter, which served as a convenient and noble pretext that ultimately delivered Lyolya from a preposterous, tiresome burden: me. Her departure came about independently, unconnected with Sergei N.'s summons—such as I understand it—but still it came as a blow to me, utterly unjustified, unprovoked, and in my more spiteful fantasies there is something telling in that: if somebody close to us deals the blow, we occasionally and more often than not forgive, but this forgiveness does not alter our new opinion of the individual, of how this person treats us (or could treat us), and only in rare cases, when we must absolve this person in all our profound sobriety, only then do we forgive wholly, but even this forgiveness is redundant, for there is no guilt of which to speak. I find it hard, and myself unwilling, to "forgive" Lyolya, and her latest wrong is destroying not only the carefree joy of my initial impressions, but also my current—albeit infrequent—imagined hopes for her. Even today—because of a scarf, perfumed with Lyolya's scent—I was gripped by an enamored, almost unconscious sense of expectation (it took me some time to realize its origin), but then I happened to remember the disdain and negligence with which she accepted that bottle of scent that I gave her, and how offended I had been then (after such excitement about the gift)—and so today's expectation has given way to the usual feelings of vengeful displeasure.

Repeatedly I pick over all the wretched trivia that provide definitive proof of Lyolya's change in attitude toward me, and this perpetual comparison of our beginning and end, which before would have been unbearable, no longer pains me but is, if anything, agreeable. But even then—in those days with Lyolya—when for the first time I discovered the sorry change, and the blow was still palpable and aching, I intentionally resorted to ever newer and more persistent tests, tests that were so often blundering and belligerent—not for the sake of hope, not from any desire to convince myself, yet again, of our tragic end, but to raise some dismal, much-needed smile inside me, one that has given rise to all these never-ending, touching comparisons. One day, at an ill-chosen moment, suddenly breaking off our previous conversation and foreknowing my imminent failure, I asked Lyolya to mend an old, blackened glove of mine. Just as I had antici-pated, she marveled at this request and replied, half-incensed: "Your concierge will do it far better than I"—and it was not difficult to discern in her irritated refusal an accompanying renunciation of any sweet concern, any solicitude for me, and moreover (hence my own outrage) a note of squeamish disgust directed specifically at the glove. I recalled that first day we spent together, my delight at her nimble handiwork and touching kindness, and how, in conducting this provocative experiment, I had poisoned that delight forever.

Even more morbidly was I struck (though now the memory is especially delectable) by Lyolya's dogged attempts to evade my favors: how she had once preened at my ardent, instinctive, chivalrous magnanimity, and how later all this seemed to her so tedious and redundant ("You're forever doing unnecessary things"—whenever I, who do not smoke, would proffer some cigarettes in their yellow wrapping, which I had bought just for her, on the off chance)—perhaps what vexed her was that it was not somebody else being so obliging.

Lyolya resisted as best she could our old mutual attentiveness, and, so as to rid herself of it, to make it officially impossible, she would not be left alone with me, the fact of which spared her not the responsibility itself (which had essentially vanished long ago), but everything that she found bothersome, everything that I have already described—the need to reciprocate, my reproachful, insistent questions—and again, despite myself, I would compare how in days past she would strive to ensure that we be together, how she would regard outsiders as enemies and, blushing with delight, cherish her every admission of care, tact, and kindness toward me. In that first month she could never have enjoyed Bobby Wilczewski's company, hitting it off with him, meeting that motley array of ludicrous, unworthy individuals, nor would she ever have fallen disappointedly, spitefully silent if an abortive date or some instruction I had bungled forced us to spend a whole evening alone together. Though I feared Lyolya's wrathful perspicacity, I proved rather deft at thwarting her wishes and shifting the blame onto others (the line would always be engaged, the Wilczewskis had gone away somewhere, it was not worth inviting Bobby today—he was with his girlfriend), and occasionally I would feel bad for

Lyolya's deceived credulity, but I much preferred this dubious (for the fear of rebuff) and rarely exploited opportunity to have our infrequent, private rendezvous—to explain myself, to question, to solicit, to torment and suffer the torments of my own unanswered rebukes.

My barrage of comparisons and would-be accusations leveled against Lyolya forever come up against others—in her favor—from the friends we have in common and, more importantly, from the time, the evenings I spent with and without her, but these comparisons, which stem only from living reality, and not from my imagination, never stimulate me or arrest me, as it were, in passing, they never enter the alluring province of "Lyolya and I," and so they prove a sober truth—that all the people around me are superfluous, that I require only Lyolya, and that I must, setting aside all this unpleasantness, go after her, secure her return and restore her lost favor. This is nigh impossible and will not happen any time soon, and I lack both the strength and the fortitude to want, to seek, to wait, and so one thing alone remains to distract and deceive me—those wonted thoughts of vengeance, the shameful joy in proofs of Lyolya's error, all that half-baked "Lyolya and I."

The most realistic and mundane experience that is still in any way available to me is the moment when, in a state of excitement, I arrive home and search for the letters that are not there but could so easily be, the letters that Lyolya might have written and ultimately (to do otherwise would be callous) will write, by hand, in her own hand, about herself and in her own words, and this anticipation, these prospective (likely cold and aloof) letters are the only thing binding me to Lyolya, the only thing that likens me to all others, people who live life, people beloved or aspiring to love, people who seem to me irresistibly worthy. And yet I have chosen for myself a different fate, the even keel of appeasement—forged from life's concessions and little, nonbinding fictions—perhaps because the fate of someone worthy and strong has not been mine, and because I no longer have a choice, or the courage to alter that choice.

I often see myself as though from without, and when I do, my purpose draws into focus, but then, how difficult and unbecoming to conquer and guard something jealously, without dreading the responsibility, a rivalry, a conflict, nor yielding to the sweet self-oblivion of sleep. Yet even as I discover my poor, unhappy predicament, I do not immediately or lightly reconcile myself to it, to failed youth, to being fated to loneliness; I obsess over the reason for my cowardice, as though some deliverance were to be found therein, and seemingly I begin to apprehend—it is difficult to put a name to and utterly impossible to eliminate; it is arguably my strongest and most intrinsic trait—that I lack that constant alternation of charge and discharge that forms the basis of every inner life and promises both respite and, thereafter, a fresh jolt into action (my first effort always demands something new); however, if I relax, then I will not be able to restrain myself, and so my accidental aspiration (these fictions about Lyolya are a case in point) will turn into an unstoppable and futile flight. My every effort will be drawn out and inevitably tiring, each distraction will lead me too far astray, and I shall find everything simple and necessary harder than others do—granted, though, my sluggish mind will manage to register and appreciate both the intense effort and the swift flight that, despite myself, overshoots its mark.

But having struck upon what predetermines my fate, a fate that is so monotonous and dull, that leads me forever away from victory and happiness, I cannot but recall some discrepancies, attempts to raise and revive me; unwittingly I compare—by dint of this new and fervent habit—my highs and lows, and with morbid curiosity I watch how slowly within me the worthy, smitten man is vanishing, the man I was when I routinely saw Lyolya, the man on whose account I would struggle and deceive, and how he is now being replaced by another—someone ordinary, placid, reserved, and no longer drawn to anything. This disappearance is taking place almost imperceptibly, and the only things that remind me of it are ridiculous, superficial trivia (my first haircut after Lyolya, a new pair of gloves instead of the old torn ones that she refused to mend) and a naïve sense of mourning for what I had with her and what was somehow connected to her, unexpected and bitter though that sense is, like a second parting. After such a conclusive split, by now quite bereft of dignity, I am transported to that most ignominious region of comparisons, wherein the supposed, the imaginary, and the real knowingly and unnecessarily merge into one: I imagine Lyolya and Sergei N. "there" and myself alone here, and it grieves me—alas, grieves and thrills me—to compare what has been so unfairly dealt us: Lyolya's preoccupation with Sergei N. and my indifference to everything, Lyolya's conviction and my jealousy, her nonchalance and my eternal searching, our so dissimilar nights, the ever-glaring disparity of success and hopeless bad luck. At the same time (crushing though it is to imagine their trysts and undoubted intimacy), for vanity's sake—for my future triumph before Lyolya—I want each of my assumptions to be proved true and accurate; I calculate, strive to remember, and am not even averse to certain underhand measures, if only to prove that I am right, and not for the first time have I tried to bolster my ineptitude for guesswork, which is so essential to carry off this internal posturing of mine, with sheer guile.

All this posturing demands of me a certain proximity to real life—it demands not only guesswork, as it does of others, but also my own active participation, and often these demands and the means of satisfying them have struck me as excessive and contradictory: I think of Lyolya (not of my own bottled-up feelings), of the idea that she may yet reciprocate, and of that terrible evening after the affair in the bistro, when it struck me that she would never love me and I allowed myself to write, but then, unexpectedly, for the very first time, I was brought closer to her. Granted, our rapprochement was passionless, consolatory—Lyolya, weary and cold, hurried me out, practically ejecting me, complaining about the late hour, and so I might have left wronged and beaten, whereas in actual fact I stood there, calm and satisfied like never before: something undeniable and important had been achieved, had miraculously come about—something that could not be taken away from me, and at long last I managed to do away with the elusiveness of fictions and assumptions, with my distrust of them, and found myself in real, proven, incontestable reality. Now I could await the advantageous equalization of my platonic friendship with Lyolya (not the equality of love, which cannot be achieved by force, but some frank, trusting, ingenuous, and friendly conversations) and with a restrained sense of impatience, without any awkwardness or annoyance—as if all that romantic uncertainty had vanished—I made ready for our next encounter, and I cannot recall another instance when a meeting after a rapprochement has been so indistinct, so like the last, so perfectly unaltered. Thereafter followed a period of painful obsession, of minute-by-minute predictions about Lyolya's current disposition toward me—yesterday, today, that very moment—and by what new and old signs I might divine this, and no longer could I, in my usual unhurried, easy way, reason with myself; I stopped recording whatever I observed and would just cling blindly to something or other quite accidental, always at random, searching for and failing to find solace or at least a relative peace of mind.

THERE IS A young lady who visits the Wilczewskis in the evenings, Ida Ivanovna Z., who is, it would seem, a Baltic German from Riga: having lived a long (and fugitive) life in Moscow, then in Berlin and in Paris, she has so muddled it all that it is no longer possible to determine her origins or the sequence of her wanderings, as if she has been stripped of her nationality—a common occurrence among Russians abroad, particularly the women. She has a milliner's workshop, opened on some small savings or borrowed money and now turning a tidy profit—the Wilczewskis speak of this with the deepest respect, and even old Wilczewski himself holds interminable discussions with her (as he does with every business-minded guest) on a means to "expand the business" with the help of one of the banks where he has "friendly connections," on Zina's joining the enterprise (in other cases it is Bobby who is tentatively proposed), but Ida Ivanovna prudently, unwaveringly, politely insists on their bringing in hard cash, which, evidently, the Wilczewskis do not have. Meanwhile, poor Zina has taken up some hat-making course and considers herself thankful for her father's constant solicitude on her behalf.

Ida Ivanovna is meek to the point of insignificance, answers questions kindly and very softly, and is never one to strike up a conversation—all this corresponds little to her appearance, which is provocative, full-blooded, and has something of the animal about it. Whenever you enter the Wilczewskis' little drawing room, Ida Ivanovna is always to be found in the corner, in an armchair, in a stiff and awkward pose—her head inclined forward, her arms folded in her lap, her legs crossed, the upper one somehow broadened, flattened, while the lower is rounded and bent—and all this, as indeed everything else about her, gives an impression of rude health, robustness, something rich and tempting. Her hands are masculine and too big, but this is made less apparent by their whiteness and manicure, and I enjoy their gentle, serene, honest grip. But when Ida Ivanovna stands and straightens herself out, she at once becomes different—as though freed of the restrictive effort to hold herself elegantly, as though forever being drawn somewhere farther down the track, and taller than one might have imagined: all people with long legs, while sitting down, seem to be shorter than they really are. I find Ida Ivanovna no sweeter or more charming than the other habitués of the Wilczewskis: there is nothing about her that might have touched or moved me, and without Lyolya, after Lyolya, although I am not searching for a touching, moving replacement, I am forever ready to be moved by somebody's feminine wiles, especially by those that resemble Lyolya's and would, as it were, prolong them, invigorate them, prop them up in my memory. This gangly and gauche woman, however, seems to be a design of contrasts: she has a broad, simple face with an energetic hook nose, soft, plump, almost tumescent lips, high cheekbones, and a plain, though pleasing, complexion—bright white and so soft, as if she has just got out of the bath. Though finding nothing "for myself" in Ida Ivanovna and scarcely sparing a thought for her after our chance encounters at the Wilczewskis', I nevertheless marked that I was glad of these chance encounters, that I would somehow set them apart and often—amid a silence or a conversation with whomever—examine her rather potent charms with that shamelessly offhand impudence that eats away at any man who has lived in Paris for a long while and cannot offend any Parisienne.

The most fortunate thing about all this was—as is usually the case for me—the absence of any obligation to act, the half-heartedness of the situation, the fact that Ida Ivanovna could not fail to mark and feel my persistent gaze, even if she did not give herself away, did not try to evade me, and only took care to adjust her skirt, which already hung below the knee—a rare modesty for such graceful, advantageous legs as hers.

This unobliging, convenient (for me), and altogether pleasant rapport was unexpectedly broken, and through no fault of my own: just the other day, at the Wilczewskis', Ida Ivanovna turned to me, as it were (she talks without altering her habitual stiff pose, and only looks directly at her *vis-à-vis* with those jaundiced, vacant, seemingly unmoving eyes of hers) and began to question me on a matter that was evidently preoccupying her:

"They say you're a man of business. My *comptable* is utterly hopeless and my accounts are in such a mess. Won't you please advise me what I'm to do?"

"It's difficult to give advice from where I'm standing—I'd have to take a look at your accounts."

"If you ever—of course, not tomorrow or even this week, but any time—find yourself free, you'd be doing me a great favor by paying me a visit. Please, I'd be ever so grateful. Otherwise, you know, I'll simply be at a loss."

"Why delay? I'll be delighted to come tomorrow."

Ida Ivanovna's invitation whipped me into action, as though I had given her my word of honor, and all of a sudden I felt that it was impossible to put the matter off. Very likely I shall never know whether it was a pretext, an "advance" (the common refrain of my student years), or whether Ida Ivanovna really had heard about me and needed my help—as with so many others who constantly monitor themselves, I completely forget that people may talk about me in my absence and what simple, unsubstantiated conclusions may be drawn from these conversations.

In any case, from this assistance in business matters, from this act of commonplace kindness, I confected for myself something joyous, and in the morning, when I awoke and, as always, became unerringly aware of my mood and the highlight of the impending day, I at once smiled inwardly and thought of Ida Ivanovna.

I had selected—not without some cunning—the approximate hour when all manner of businesses close, hoping that the staff and milliners would disperse with my appearance, and that I would be invited into the proprietress's living quarters, which were located on the premises (a fact that had been mentioned one day at the Wilczewskis' and which I had half-consciously registered and committed to memory). My first impression of the atelier was a glimpse of bare arms belonging to the young female workers, who were elegant and carefree in that Parisian way, among whom the proprietress stood out, and whom she dominated—like the prima donna in an opera—with her height and forceful appearance, which however remained (as in her unassuming corner at the Wilczewskis') expectantly silent, a little absent and abashed. Her arms were also bared to the shoulders: strong, slender, and so soft to the touch that I had the urge to reach out and caress them there and then.

It happened exactly as I had expected, or, rather, as I had calculated and engineered—I know from long experience that easily won success is not in my lot, that I must myself encourage events and gerrymander my fortune—and this time Ida Ivanovna, as though executing my plans, asked me to wait while the workers dispersed, before leading me into her spotless dining room, where after some inconspicuous efforts she treated me to tea and jam—*à la russe*—and to French liqueurs of various colors in sparkling crystal decanters.

Directly after tea we set about tackling the ledgers—I can, by suppressing my primordial laziness, bring myself to the necessary state of intense effort required for work and remain there for long periods, continuing all the while to suppress my impatient desire to return to my former lazy inertia, and then (insofar as possible) I will delve into the work assigned to me, after which—because of luck or praise, like a diligent first-rate pupil—I will light up with inspiration and often, impatient and at the same time focused, achieve more than I myself could have hoped for or expected. Much to my pride and pleasure, I found some obvious errors in the accounts, but more importantly I balanced the books for the previous year. Ida Ivanovna tried to explain to me a great number of things that I did not immediately comprehend, beginning, as it were, from afar and in an uncertain tone of voice, but so sensibly, with such an ingenuous disclosure of her apparently remarkable commercial ventures, that I felt sorry for her, for her lack of success, and my own affairs were cast as unworthy amateurism. After an hour and a half's work, Ida Ivanovna, grateful and as though emboldened by my cooperation and success, bid me occupy myself while she quickly fixed "a little something for dinner."

"I'll be terribly hurt if you don't stay."

She brought vodka, cognac, expensive caviar, some salads, and as I looked at the table, decked with all these tempting articles, I marveled, roused as though from hibernation, from my long exertion, and already rejoicing that tedium and work were at an end, that now came the reward, deserved, happy, with untold possibilities, supper and afterward these untold possibilities, and I began to feel so perfectly fine, so instantly renewed, as though my abandonment of the previous weeks, the clinging to the past, to Lyolya's specter, all that constant melancholic glancing over my shoulder had never been, and an unexpected childish primal joy set in, the one that makes us jump and run, the one that we dub gratuitous and whose cause is often discovered without difficulty: that being somebody's arrival, one's own return to rude health, impending pleasure, the warm spring sun. Unexpectedly, Ida Ivanovna had dressed up for the occasion and entered the room radiant, fresh, and with charming, insincere apologies that she had had to let the maid go and that instead of dinner there would be "a cold and frugal supper." Intoxicated even before I had touched the vodka, I watched Ida Ivanovna—not as I did at the Wilczewskis', but quite brazenly, in the sure expectation of her responsiveness, as though having arranged beforehand that she would be drawn into the game (in such cases I know I wear an obnoxious, triumphant smile, one that I cannot suppress). To my surprise, Ida Ivanovna maintained a contemplative restraint, a kind of unwitting dignity—true, one that no longer put up any resistance, yet this untimely dignity prevented my unravelling entirely, my casting off all humanity and scrupulousness, my deeming every one of my desires—a monstrously shameful thing—to be instantly practicable and necessarily given fiat; in short, it halted my inflamed rudeness, which forever required some conspiratorial, almost larcenous, consent, while at the same time it animated me, it eased and inspired my merry intoxication. The vodka, the rich red wine, the liqueurs—all this took its toll little by little, but in such inebriety (not the lonely sort, without despair or expectation) I find there to be an incomparable loveliness and, dare I say it, an unquestionable advantage: not only does it dispense with my memories of myself, with this constant awareness of my own reality, this prying mistrust of everything, but it also does away with the awareness of any awkwardness in external situations, as it does the awareness of any intimacy, of any toe-curling proximity—had I been sober, I should not have been able to forget what an incongruous pair Ida Ivanovna and I made, that she is tall, hefty, no longer youthful, and possessed of a somehow bovine, obtusely melancholic nature, while I look like a boy and ought or want to present myself as sardonic and aloof, that she and I are irretrievably alien to one another, and that we simply cannot be side by side, I should have been ashamed of my friendly, quasi-amorous tone, but there you have it—after all that I had drunk, there was neither any awkwardness nor impediment, and I do not recall how we wound up in the bedroom, atop that wide double bed, or how I, having cozily nestled up to Ida Ivanovna, with the faint brush of half-parted lips kissed her tender shoulder, which was revealed by degrees and suddenly freed, like a separate, animated concentration of blinding light and warmth. Taking her obedient fingers, excessively big and powerful as they are, and her wary, almost weightless palm, I caressed my own cheeks (rejoicing at my forethought to have shaven) and reveling in the provision of these rare hours and, in a different way—feebly, almost imperceptibly—in the possibility of some support. Suddenly Ida Ivanovna broke free and, with a significant look (voluptuous, almost cruel, her eyes dark and moist), at last having transformed herself into my shameless accomplice, quietly and insinuatingly whispered, "I'll be just a moment, my dear," before leisurely disappearing somewhere. A few minutes later she reappeared from the bathroom (obviously taking care to avoid the other rooms), slowly parted the draperies, and touchingly, all but theatrically, leaned forward, for some reason shielding her face with her hands—in a state of complete undress, shapelier and more slender than I had imagined, "*fausse-forte*" to coin an expression. Then, with a curiously solemn gesture, she flicked a switch, leaving only the reflected light of the bathroom, and rushed toward me, silent, unsmiling, and not quite fathomable. She took me firmly in her arms—so firmly in fact that I could not breathe— but I (from male instinct or experience) tried to push her off, to overpower her, to exhaust her, and, scarcely having demonstrated my cool dominance over her, I took her in my own arms tenderly and firmly, remaining perfectly still, as though resting, as though regretting her fatigue, delighting in our prodigious union, in the ostensibly magical power of the embrace, which always thrills me—to the point of fright.

As so often in such moments, I was able to reason freely, though confusedly, with myself, and a bright flash of bewilderment struck me as I wondered why I had never felt so impeccably assured with Lyolya; equally bewildering was the logical conclusion that love is not to be found in a carnal or sexual "match" alone and is even frequently incompatible with it. Stirred thus by recollections of Lyolya, succumbing to age-old resentments, I mused (as I had done before) that her rejection, a constant and glaring source of bitterness to me, was to blame for everything, but in that same instant Ida Ivanovna took it upon herself to speak of Lyolya for the first time—half-jealously—and just then I sensed the approaching, disinhibiting danger of my customary heartache for Lyolya, so I had to dismiss those sharp, clear thoughts and all this unnecessary talk at once, brushing them aside indignantly. Nonetheless, my pleasure was tinged with a slightly bitter note, much too insignificant to spoil it but sufficient enough to ruffle it, and so my enjoyment, compounded by this bitterness, proved subtly and, as it were, cruelly tender. When I woke from my stupor, however, now sober, I had the irresistible urge to leave (how different it was with Lyolya—flight after intimacy is an irrefutable proof of love's absence), and I set about persuading Ida Ivanovna that I should not be able to get up in the morning, that I feared "compromising" her, that the Wilczewskis might infer something, and so in the end poor Ida Ivanovna, frightened, bewildered, drove me out herself.

"Pity. I thought you might stay the night. When will I see you again?"

"Tell you what: I'll telephone, if I may."

June 23

YESTERDAY I LACKED the mental stamina, was simply too lazy to bother with the usual exertions required to describe everything that happened, everything that I felt after the evening with Ida Ivanovna. I left her and forgot about her instantly, vaguely conscious of some conceited triumph of mine, glad that I had not obliged myself in any way to her, had not agreed to another meeting, glad of my freedom and the languorous, immaculate slumber that lay ahead. It was still early, and the warmth was balmy, as it is in summer; there were people about, people in no rush to go anywhere, enjoying their leisure and a humble stroll through the city, lonely latecomers like me, and, hidden on benches, enamored couples would loom out of the dark, frozen in a blissful stasis—I am always astonished how many happily loving people there are, how many flagrant displays of happy love one encounters, how rarely this happens to me and how my own experiences, rare though they are, seem so incomparably lofty, casting a radiance over my other, ordinary, lackluster days. As I continued to marvel at the happy nocturnal couples, not envying them in the least, I could not help thinking of

Lyolya and inevitably imagined myself with her, and the scrap of nature that one distinguishes in Paris—the darkling clearings of verdure, the odd streaks of sky between roofs and trees, delicate, beneficent, perhaps even remotely forbidding, and the almost living, caressing, gently enswathing warmth— this scrap of nature reconstituted another, real, nature, one so overflowing with love and so powerful that one can but surrender to it, that one must, submissively and compliantly, love and sweetly be loved. My feelings for Lyolya momentarily swelled to infinite proportions and made me, without making any allowance for failure, wish ardently for the only possible means of her incarnation—a letter: no sooner had I thought of this than I was instantaneously transported to a long-familiar realm (that of feverish epistolary anticipation); I recognized it at once by its telltale signs and re-enacted it, until I stumbled upon something new, a situation that I had never before encountered—that for the first time I had not gone home for a whole day and, hence, there had been three posts and thrice the ordinary chance of a letter; what was more, I had "betrayed" Lyolya, someone had taken a fancy to me, just as someone else had to her, we were "quits," and I would read this, today's sought-for and undoubted letter from Lyolya, on even terms.

In the event, it was a miracle of coincidence, as though fate had begun to push me in the way of success and action, to prove that something could be achieved, and so I was less surprised by the letter than I had been by that other, prior coincidence—when Ida Ivanovna, as though in reply to my fleeting thoughts about Lyolya, had suddenly begun to talk of her.

I examined the envelope and its address like a rare gift (delivered into my hands at long last and so, admittedly, having already lost a little of its value), and, like a spoiled child, I pitied myself and my homecomings—those that had gone before and the many that were yet to come—when such a letter would not be waiting for me, and so, without rushing, without guessing at the content and tone of the letter, tempering my reckless inclinations, I tore open the envelope— Lyolya wrote cordially, a dash excitedly, and I immediately understood that she was not writing out of duty, but wanted to discuss a great many things and somehow to reckon with me anew. The letter was—contrary to my expectation—not addressed from Berlin: Sergei N. has invited Lyolya and Katerina Viktorovna to W. just outside Dresden, and lodged them together in a small country house, while installing himself in a *pension*. Lyolya did not hide her disappointment—I have always been astonished by the courage of her confessions, her ability to overcome, to overpower her sense of *amour-propre* and, without excessive, ostentatious self-abasement, to tell the truth. She writes: "Sergei and I cannot be together, Aunt Katya is with us constantly, and in the evening, after some music, Sergei sends me home, lest there be any awkwardness in front of her. I think he has arranged all this on purpose. Generally speaking, he treats me as he did on that day when our relationship ended, but now, as then, I cannot be certain that he doesn't love me. To think, I asked him why it ended and even tried to prompt him, talking about art, the need for freedom, and his sacrifice at the time, but he changed the subject in disgust. Am I really never to know?" I detected in Lyolya's letter not only a note of disappointment in Sergei N.'s attitude to her, but also in Sergei N. himself, and, instinctively rushing to divine everything and make flippant generalizations, I immediately decided that Sergei N. had both sensed his own blunder with Lyolya and tried, with the help of Katerina Viktorovna, to protect himself from any worries or temptations. No sooner had I decided that Lyolya was somehow "reckoning" with me and that Sergei N. had "bungled it" than I found myself immovably calm; nothing that Lyolya said or did could hurt me now—I was impervious to those artificially roused, pointed recollections that were once so insulting and so often hurtful. This strange, well-noted, paradoxical human trait—to draw attention through indifference and to repel it through displays of ardor or kindness—exists not only in love, where it is indisputable, but also in every other human endeavor, and so often in politics, in art, in business even, the successful ones are those who are indifferent, or feign indifference, to their métier. This inscrutable general propensity offends—especially in the case of love—my perhaps naïve striving for perfection, for transparent incorruptibility, and my reluctance to "play the game," and I console myself with the idea that there is a higher tier of love where this trait vanishes—we, people without God and without faith, need something palpably alive at least to invest it with divinity and lofty perfection, and we unwittingly sanctify those rare days and hours of love's reciprocity, of which we write and talk, as do the faithful of hours of prayer. And yet, as I recall in all good conscience, my own such days, so astonishing and never to be repeated, I seem unable to apprehend that strange trait, to discern that push and pull of the contradictory (truly, it does run its course and vanish), and perhaps this higher tier of love—devoid of miserable human frailty—is neither my own invention nor a comfort, and it is only my habitual mistrust of everything exalted in me that brings me to talk of consolation.

I no longer wished to think about Lyolya, and so my obsessive attention to her was transferred onto Sergei N., whose fate, like mine, seems suddenly more familiar to me than all my wasted feelings for Lyolya, which have lost their hold and vibrancy. Such miracles of temporary loss or the definitive end to robust and seemingly powerful emotions always strike me as an especially tragic imperfection of ours, yet another proof of our cruel inconstancy; I am trying to unravel this and make it clear to myself—but I fear that my understanding is simplistic and much too arbitrary: to me, love seems to be the development of a stubborn, basic, and undoubtedly touching ambition, one that constitutes the essence, the whole sense, the "idea" of any romantic relationship, which is destroyed when that very ambition disappears;

the ambition, the "idea," the sense of my first love for Lyolya was my faith in her benevolent support, in our mutual support for one another, the kind that is natural in those who have suffered greatly and for that reason understand each other; later came another "idea"—how unlike the former it was—one that, without my noticing, became habitual and convenient, a kind of voluptuous abandonment, a resentment of Sergei N.'s favor, but now Lyolya's unexpectedly agreeable letter has broken that familiar, sweet resentment, and nothing has come to take its place. I have yet to find within myself some psychological echo of those contrived, artificial thoughts about Lyolya, but on the other hand I have understood, have simply recognized in Sergei N. my own lingering and unduly deceived expectations: never before have we enjoyed such similarity in our respective situations; I once envied his five-year intimacy with Lyolya; back then—not without condescension—I looked upon myself as his happy successor, but only now, since this letter, have I been overwhelmed by bouts of sympathy and burning curiosity, which is driven by some sort of diabolical affinity for my rival, by the prospect of having it out with him, as I have never done with any other. For so long I failed to see such a rival in Sergei N., one who arouses my curiosity and in whom I share an inadvertent kinship, for I have neither met him, nor had any direct confrontation with him, for it is not nagging, loathsome jealousy that has been drawing me to him, nor is it conciliatory (in the wake of jealousy and victory) forgiveness, but yesterday our sorry resemblance was suddenly revealed to me, and in that moment a pity—the very same that I lavish upon myself—was born of our kinship, and so, giving myself free rein, cutting loose and running wild, I imagined endless conversations filled with mutual admiration, conversations predicated on a sense of despair that was allayed by the spiritual depths that we both of us possessed.

These imaginary conversations, the possibility of such a meeting, seemed all the more pleasing to me since I had always maintained (because of all that I knew about Sergei N. or else had gathered from Lyolya) a perfectly singular attitude toward him—that of the semienamored devotion we so readily feel for those to whom we necessarily or voluntarily submit (or for those to whom we should like to submit) and who as a rule simply do not notice us. This boundless devotion is of course in no way obligatory—indeed, how often it is precisely the reverse—yet it does serve as the basis, or rather even the impetus, for the many movements of our psyche, which guide us toward the powerful, and which betray an elusive though indisputable uniformity: the doggish devotion to the hand that pushes it away; the benediction of a tormentress who cares nothing for us; the confession (even if fictitious) of a criminal before a judge who is just and "understands all"; the facelessness of first-rate soldiers, who blend, as it were, into their commanding officer-cum-father; the faith schoolboys hold in the wisdom of a favorite teacher; the hero-worship of a sovereign, at times even of noblemen or plutocrats, from which loyalty and snobbism arise—these are but some haphazardly named incarnations of that same undiscriminating devotion, and for each of us it is captivating beyond compare to imagine just reward and praise for all this unbridled devotion, for all our efforts and pains. Within me this loyal semienamorment is joined—out of latent, brazen self-conceit—by a mad hope, that my ennobling parity with some magnifico to whom I have been devoted, that my merited, rightful superiority before all others, will at last be recognized: when I used to imagine conversations with Sergei N., it was this rather lifeless, never-yet-realized triumph of mine that I envisaged, but now my level-pegging with him seems to me so thrillingly assured (this must be the same thrill that a military commander experiences on the eve of certain victory: just a few days more, and then—glory). My unmistakable parity with Sergei N. becomes all the clearer and more incontestable to me: we both of us chose Lyolya, both of us lost her, and we both, with equal reconciliation, bore this irreparable loss; we share the same history, the same—hidden from all, understood by us both, equally heroic—outcome. There is yet another winning (at least, as far as I am concerned) trait that unites us in some meaningful way: I am moved, both in myself and in others, by unshakeable, lasting feelings, by everything that is illumined as the years pass by, and how glorious it is to find that what matters most to me burns slowly and lasts for so long: such is the case with my imaginary novel, dreamed up in childhood and still having those same characters and relationships, with my endless patience for Lyolya, which was eventually crowned with love—is this not the same level on which Sergei N.'s stubborn love for Lyolya exists? A love that survived their estrangement, her marriage, his segue from obscurity to fame and recognition, which might have altered everything about a man. To all appearances, his so perfect love has not been diminished by this current rejection (surely instituted by me), but this rejection suddenly seems—of course, from here, from afar—not entirely like mine, which was always cowardly, bound for the pain of humiliation, but somehow sublimely tragic, which would have suited me marvelously, and so I see anew, with more lenience and dignity, my own recent past, and am already certain of an estimable and artful future. Now from Sergei N. I return to Lyolya, to Lyolya and me, and find myself once again with but one wish—ardent, unassuming, unattainable— that of Lyolya's immediate presence, of being sated by that presence.

June 26

B EFORE THE ARRIVAL of Lyolya's letter, I believed (after all my unanswered appeals to the void) that writing my reply would be a glad occasion. It unexpectedly transpires, however, that I find it just as tedious to fill the statutory four pages, just as necessary to overcome myself, as with any other obligatory task standing before me: clearly there is something lingering from my newfound, dispiriting semiconfidence in Lyolya, but then my days, more to the point, are filled with little events that distract and divert me— only yesterday, with relative ease, I concluded a large and complex business deal, and even now I am stunned by all the money, the purchases, the assurance of material well-being, the emboldened expectations for the future. Queer how at a time ostensibly demanding confidences and ingenuous friendly outpourings I am able to content myself alone or with chance acquaintances and drinking companions—I suppose this way I exhibit neither the vanity nor the usual poses of bright-eyed triumph or gloomy resignation; perhaps my spiritual core exists above and beyond the boom and bust of business.

Just yesterday, toward evening—after two solitary days without any obligations that might otherwise have justified my idleness—I suddenly realized that I could put it off no longer and forced myself to write the most rational and detailed response I could muster. Soon enough, however, I got carried away, and the result was a feverish missive—at long last I could satisfy my unforgotten grievances, bearing into reality all my lengthy quarrel with Lyolya, which until now had been imaginary and devoid of purpose. What I really wanted (beastly though it was) was to hurt Lyolya, to crush her mercilessly by pointing out—in a friendly way, of course—that in a position such as hers, one so patently desperate and absurd, she could not remain forcibly bound to Sergei N., could not remain dependent on him financially and not look for a way out. I was in fact furious at the thought that Lyolya had sacrificed me for the sake of this "situation." If only, with words that were pure and courageous, I had prevented this, fought it, assuming responsibility for all my rebukes; but out of caution, or feigned delicacy, I preferred to avail myself of another stratagem, one so typical of many, which consists in alluding to the opinion of others (presumed or imagined) and, under that protection, uttering all the poisonous, dangerous, wicked things that I could otherwise neither say nor write. (A common enough formula: I myself am tolerant and broad-minded, but just think of your parents—in other instances, friends, critics, jurors—they won't see eye to eye and will argue the following . . .) I invoked Katerina Viktorovna's undoubted objection: "The poor woman. I can just imagine how embarrassed she must feel, how awkward it must be for her to witness your relations and to be made to partake in them herself—and what with her sense of independence and those old-fashioned sensibilities of hers." Of my own dissatisfaction I wrote with restraint—that, being so far away, I could not judge, that from the very day of her departure I had resolved not to interfere, that, when all is said and done, I trust her judgments in those trickier moments— and in a few brief words I described my days, and, as so often happens, I recounted only the most recent events that cast me in a worthy light: "I meet nobody and desire to see no one; but I am never bored by myself. The Wilczewskis, whom I have not visited in a long while, have always been very good and attentive to me. Tell me, ought I to try my luck with Zina? She has been awfully kind to me and is clearly bored on her own."

I cannot recall why I made such a boastful and false innuendo—so as to tease Lyolya or for some other not entirely clear, esoteric reason: I have, where such observations are concerned, a curious habit whereby I never allow myself to "fictionalize" (unless, of course, the observations themselves are deliberate lies)—every "fictitious," casually dropped observation about myself, which I later regret and would rather destroy and take back, always comes true in the end, as though life itself provides the missing material and, in so doing, salvages my precarious honesty, or as though I see so very much that fails to reach my insufficiently observant consciousness, only for it to be revealed to me later in my own words which seem so like another's. All this came to me because of that remark about Zina—a remark that was arbitrary, yet as ever proved right in the end.

Lately, as I mentioned to Lyolya in my letter, I have not paid the Wilczewskis a single visit, fearing an encounter with Ida Ivanovna; my feelings for her are not at all honorable or chivalrous, as they were for Lyolya and as they still are, in my naïve fantasies, for any another woman. It is true that sometimes—especially at night, when haunted by visions of Ida Ivanovna looking just as she did on that drunken evening—I lament my solitude and find myself suddenly wanting to be with her, as she surrenders to me and gives in to love, but come morning this desire always vanishes: in the light of day, out in public and in the midst of work, it is the sober, long-divined awareness of our incompatibility, of the need to hide our shameful rapprochement, that must inevitably win out; if only it were possible to meet for the sake of immediate gratification, without all those tedious and insincere overtures—"Like animals," as mothers disdainfully educate their curious sons—how many strong, long-lasting bonds there would be, how many women's pride would be spared. Yet I find simply intolerable all these obligatory overtures and this show of intimacy (or else, that I should be made vainly to seek out that intimacy from some ingrained sense of gentlemanliness) for a woman to whom I am emotionally indifferent; instead, I put off the promised telephone calls and the calculatedly fortuitous meetings, taking my elusiveness to the point of outright defiance, to the point whereby it is impossible to remedy the situation or to undertake anything without some inadvertent nudge from without. But it just so happened that Bobby provided exactly this.

He arrived just as I was rereading my (on the face of it) scrupulously honest and (essentially) vindictive letter to Lyolya. As I nodded my approval of the missive, he began to chide me in a friendly sort of way for my recent neglect.

"It's a bit rum of you just to drop off the face of the earth like that. Zina's ever so cross with you, you know. She gave me orders to bring you back forthwith. How have you been anyway? All work and no play?"

In abstraction, I examined his light summer necktie, done in a devil-may-care manner but without a single crease, his pastel silk shirt and the deliberately mismatched suit that hung on him like a sack—it was all gaily colored and terribly expensive, and, as always, I was taken aback and not a little envious, wondering where he had got his hands on the money for it. He perused the few books I had and dutifully marveled at something else entirely:

"You have all of Pushkin, you lucky thing. How I adore Pushkin. He has such *lapidary* lines. Do you recall *The Egyptian Nights*? I really must introduce you to L. Such an erudite chap, as you can't even begin to imagine."

Bobby stood there, full pleased with the daintiness of his turn of phrase (as it happens, "erudite" is another favorite and oft-repeated word of his), and, deciding that he had proved himself well enough, turned to more prosaic matters:

"All the same, I simply cannot fathom how it is that you can live in such sparse and dreary (he meant to say 'dilapidated') rooms. With all your means, you ought to set yourself up somewhere much grander than this. In any case, grab your hat. You're not going to give me the slip this time."

We set out together, arm in arm (not without a certain cunningness has Bobby befriended and ingratiated himself with me), and along the way we chatted about women.

"A charming specimen, that Ida Ivanovna. The poor thing's caught cold and has been cooped up indoors lately. Do you suppose she has anybody?"

I was relieved to learn that I would not encounter her at the Wilczewskis', that I should be spared an evening of rebuke, albeit tacit. Cheered immeasurably by this, I began to point out some of the young ladies coming toward us and, like schoolboys, we arrogantly discussed their advantages and disadvantages and, most importantly, tried to divine what their appearance concealed: that one has down over her lip—I doubt she'd look good taking off her stockings or showing her bare arms; look at the way that one's blouse quivers as she walks—her chest must be uneven; and that one, look how straight her dress hangs—she must have a low waist; on the contrary, it's those flat shoes of hers—she has fearlessly long legs. . . . It would be impossible to enumerate all those inane attributes; it feels strange even to have picked up on them and to call them by their name after my long inattention to such things because of Lyolya. My dealings with Ida Ivanovna have changed me, and it is as if I have begun to see things clearly: sometimes a novel experience, however insignificant, is enough to jolt our memory and make us perceive afresh the similarities, and all this leaves us, as it were, precipitously enriched. There is something else that Ida Ivanovna has bequeathed me: I now find it easy to judge and think about other women, because some long-standing barrier between them and me has diminished, vanished almost; they now seem more intelligible, more approachable, closer, in a word, as though I have managed to retain that winning, enchanting sense of ease that Ida Ivanovna would acquire after a little wine and that has spread to all women, and as though this sense of ease has granted me not only confidence in my own success—on account of my vainglorious memories—but even the success itself, that mysterious capacity to excite, which before I would impotently and sorrowfully find only in others, and which back in Lyolya's days was probably still hindered by my constant lack of freedom. With this new-found confidence, with a vague sense of hope, I arrived at the Wilczewskis', where Zina met me with her usual languorous and all-encompassing, "Well, what do you have to say for yourself?"—while somebody (apparently the "erudite chap," L.) answered deftly on my behalf: "Guilty as charged but deserving of leniency."

At the Wilczewskis' it was, as always (and despite their worldly pretensions), noisy and shambolic, guests sitting in various attitudes, each group absorbed in its own affairs and seeming a nuisance to the others. I realized, one way or another, that I should easily be able to constitute such a separate, solitary little group with Zina, and her tacit consent, along with this immediate clarity—forgoing any tiresome or tedious pains—added to the cheery confidence that had brought me there and was gradually flourishing because of all these successively favorable circumstances—the postponement of my encounter with Ida Ivanovna, Zina's alarming, half-encouraging "consent," my sudden freedom from Lyolya, a freedom that was not definitive, resembling as it did a reprieve and having begun at that very moment when Ida

Ivanovna took a fancy to me and I began to hope for something from her (yet another proof of my correct and well-founded jealousy of Lyolya's success, of her desire to be liked—a fleeting, accidental thought, but one that nevertheless poisoned my happy inspiration just a touch, one that single-handedly reminded me of the long and shameful time that I spent obsessing over Lyolya, full of resentment for her and unceasing fearful devotion to her).

Zina seemed to me a changed woman—no longer her usual pallid gray and a little awkward, but rosier somehow, proud and elegant in her bearing, and wearing a pair of pointed, pinching, patent-leather heels. She strode up to me in an unaccountably cheerful mood, and I found it so charming—in sharp distinction to Ida Ivanovna, probably on account of her age and appearance—to have her by my side, holding her warm, tightly clasped palm in my hand. We ensconced ourselves in a corner and talked about the inevitable—to women like Zina (those who lack that glint, who are seen through at once) I always speak with a kind of inner disdain, ignoring them and never answering for my own words—Zina was evidently not listening to me, and she just smiled with her intoxicated, distant, suggestive eyes while she stroked (almost caressed) her slender legs with her beautiful, strong fingers, arousing herself as she did so—and, what was more, her arousal was immediately transmitted to me. That seemingly absent-minded feminine manner, that very gesture of one leg thrown over the other, squeezing it tightly as though in an embrace, contains both an invitation and a dangerous, attractive hope. I sat there beside Zina while she played the quiet ingénue (just as before), and I knew that I could not leave her there with the others, that if I did not stay, then I should lose a unique opportunity for a bit of easy male luck—thus, occasionally, on a tram or in the underground, do you spot in the eyes of your accidental neighbor an alluring promise, without any guile, and from a sense of embarrassment, from a sense of terror that others might notice, you unexpectedly, with a feeling of shame and disappointment, get off at your intended, murderously early stop. But perhaps I was destined not to give up, but to keep going—doggedly, boorishly, primitively (less and less do I find myself impeded by considerations of decorum or delicacy)—and so, after the guests had stood up and said their good-byes, I nonchalantly, without the least inhibition, thinking of one thing only, to win, and to this end trying to be as natural and convincing as possible, asked Zina:

"You don't look very tired. I'm not, either. Why don't we sit here some more and continue our little chat."

She gave me the faintest of smiles.

"Very well, but let me see to Papa and tidy up first."

Bobby retired to his room—the siblings never get in each other's way—leaving Zina and me in that little parlor. She lay down on the daybed, and a decisive moment came when I, apropos of nothing, boldly and without pretext, moved over to this daybed as well. Then, intuitively, without any stratagem, hitting upon some convenient and long-familiar formula, I took her hands in mine (or, rather, I took possession of them), ticklingly scratched the silk of her stockings, leaned in and kissed her neck, grazing her soft, delicate chin, before suddenly—surprising even myself—overwhelming her, marveling at the cruelty of my weight and the impossibility for her to free herself and push me away. At that moment, she whispered, "Careful! Papa," (women are more accustomed to fear than we are, and they have such instincts that we cannot hope to grasp), and no sooner had I moved to one side and adopted a more respectable position, than old Wilczewski appeared at the door, unshaven, wearing cheap, threadbare slippers (not intended for guests) and carrying a French newspaper.

"Time for bed, Zina dear," he softly intoned. "You must be tired."

As I left, I lamented—on account of my masculine vanity—my dashed good fortune, though I considered it secured and postponed only for a short period of time: I had grown so coarse that I was no longer ashamed of myself, nor did I feel any guilt before Zina or her father, who had doubtless divined everything and, dare I say, as a father, as a man belonging to another generation, must have felt gravely and terribly offended by my behavior. I consoled myself with the compellingly simple argument so typical of my generation—"She is a grown woman and knows what she wants and is free to act as she pleases"—after which I calmed down and immediately forgot about her.

I also reflected—smugly and with surprise—on the varied and active life that I now enjoy, when before it had seemed so imperviously humdrum: easy success in business, two women fussing over me, to say nothing of the need to be devious and cunning, which my sense of indifference finds agreeable. Indifference, however, is what I feel most of all these days, perhaps alongside an awareness of novelty: the recent past may remain uniquely close and be mine alone, yet it was also feeble, blind, poor, and at times devastatingly humiliating.

July 5

M Y "ACTIVE" LIFE continues, but it is not what I naïvely imagined it to be—it lacks the anticipated thrill of movement, of success, of being able to give orders and comfortably, without rushing, to discuss what really changes from suchlike discussions; it lacks those touching, thrilling, deliberately withheld delights that feelings and hints of feelings entail (whether they are happy or sad is unimportant): somehow or other I must see the day through to evening, trying to dodge the many tedious or irrelevant people, and those two women (without giving myself airs, there could be more of them), giving them the slip and dreaming up pretexts to avoid seeing them, to put off our latest assignation and to remain alone for a single, solitary hour more—I have not yet the strength to escape all this, to finish with it once and for all, or, rather, I have not yet decided anything: it will be easy for me to act on my decision, for I have not been drawn into this present, as it were, alien, life, and I am not inextricably bound by it to anyone. And yet it goes on, robbing me of my time, and there is nothing to take its place: what I dread more than anything is an empty, unallocated day.

I am, essentially, still tied up with Lyolya; everything to do with her, all those imaginary rebukes, slights, and hopes remain, but they are somehow muted, frozen by the cold and excessive tranquility of this internally static "active life," devoid as it is of that ordinary irrepressible spirit, and often I must artificially muster the requisite indignation or tenderness to escape the tedium and ascertain whether I have not become too numbed. I often receive Lyolya's sweet, considerate, solicitous letters—these pertain to my active, real, unimaginary relations—and, as before, I wait for them impatiently, but with a new, circumspect sangfroid: hence, if I myself compose a particularly touching or successful letter, I immediately envisage Lyolya's grateful reaction, I long to know it with palpable accuracy, and in the interim—until I receive a response—I even prefer not to find a familiar white envelope on my desk.

Lyolya continues to have trouble with Sergei N., but still she hesitates to leave him. I, too, find my circumstances unchanged—as though jaded by both women, I wearily, sometimes with a predatory, instantly extinguished sense of anticipation, await now Zina, now Ida Ivanovna, and I am even accustomed—at the Wilczewskis', when they are together—to their petty, acrimonious squabbling, to the never-ending barbs, the sudden, squalling half declarations—made out of spite—and to my own cowardly, neutral politeness as I continue to feign ignorance. Far too often, when the evening is nearly over—after the obligatory boring farewells—I unwittingly find myself at Ida Ivanovna's. She is disillusioned with me and, in her naïveté, has revealed to me her original designs: "Every business needs a man, you know." Having realized once and for all that I shall never be that man in her business, that my help has been incidental and mercenary, that I was, so to speak, lumbered with her, she no longer insists, and only occasionally does she seek my advice or beseechingly bring me her confused ledgers, although she cannot understand my apathy: this (and her scornful jealousy for Zina) inevitably piques her, but what matters is that she has accepted the terms of our agreement—like a man, without regrets, and having, as it were, "weathered the storm"—and I suspect that she has decided, with a business-like acumen, not to let me go, not to bother finding a replacement, lest she happen to land upon someone shady and disreputable. Ida Ivanovna strikes me as one of those women who will faithfully "work at a lover," if they deem him to be superior to themselves in some way, and who will then take pride in the tendernesses that they have bought, but which seem somehow earned. Their demands are limited to a bit of help in business, which they find so touching and which binds their lovers a little, but it so happens that these women often come a cropper—more often, in fact, than others: they are taken in with skillful persistence by wicked idlers and men of dubious and even criminal nature, and, owing to this difficult experience—their own and that of others—they constantly fear everything. I do not measure up to Ida Ivanovna's sentimental expectations, but then she is safe with me.

No emotional intimacy has developed between us: neither do I listen to, nor do I recall, her tales—which usually entail resentment and regret—because of their deplorable wretchedness, because of their absurd straightforwardness, and, perhaps, because of Ida Ivanovna's distinctly un-Russian patter; often I simply cut her off with an unabashed, rude, unambiguous gesture, to which she does not object, smiling docilely with her instantly moist, muddy eyes.

My relationship with Zina is a far more complex affair and, in a sense, it matters more to me. It lacked, almost from the very outset, that pleasing game of flirtation that I played with Ida Ivanovna, and—although I am not in the least hurt by this, although Zina irritates me even more than Ida Ivanovna and is forever artless in the extreme—I still weigh my words, deem it necessary to pity and indulge, and I restrain myself in many respects. Such exaggerated solicitude, which clearly does not correspond to my actual indifference toward Zina, has sprung from a trifle, the memory of which is more wounding than the actual event that caused it and immediately took its place. One evening, soon after that memorable night at the Wilczewskis' (with my clumsy and degrading failure), Zina paid me an unexpected visit, spent an age waiting for me in our *pension*'s "salon" (I returned home later than she had anticipated), and then, in my room upstairs—without resistance, without pretense—she gave herself to me fully, as it were, silently clinging to me and seemingly surprised by the impetuosity that she encountered from me. I had not managed to wake up from the drowsy fatigue of the day and was both exhilarated and aroused like never before by this sudden transition, but just as inexplicably quickly, I cooled, sobered up, and hurried under some pretext to send Zina packing, while she, still aflame, ashamed, hiding and stroking her naked, practically waled shoulder (into which only a moment ago, having torn off her blouse, I had been boorishly burying my face), with the indignant conviction of a child, bawled straight at me—as usual, with borrowed, clichéd words:

"Oh, you nasty man! Wicked, wicked man!"

I sensed, however, that these borrowed words expressed her righteous indignation and constituted an indictment (one that I deserved, on account of my foolish greed), and they moved me to a feeling of repugnance for myself: I could not let Zina go without putting things right, without satisfying myself (even if I was forced to overplay my hand) that she had forgiven me or else had treated me unjustly.

"Why wicked? I don't want to risk riling you, but you don't love me any more than I love you. Our relations are friendly, free of ambition and grudges—why are you so determined to complicate them?"

"Friendly? If that's what you call it. I would never have come here if I didn't love you. You know that perfectly well. By all accounts, I expected better of you, and I was well within my rights to do so."

Then, trying to envisage clearly our recent conversations in the presence of others, I recalled those much too irresponsible, so reassuringly kind looks that I had given her, the slow and gentle squeezing or suggestive kissing of a hand, my bitter surprise at her cold and saddening words, my hasty intercessions in arguments to win her warm and trusting gratitude—everything that each of us so easily and imperceptibly squanders (from loneliness, from a sense of spiritual malaise, from the habitual desire to please or be chronically obliging) and that an innocent, dreamy woman like Zina, one given to exaggeration, can take, and is entitled to take, for something more. No matter how I tried, I could not find any comforting—even for a while—ruse (I do sometimes have such attacks of uncharacteristic sincerity), and, as I said good-bye, I pressed myself expiatorily to Zina's cheek, which was wet with tears, using all the little artifice that I could muster, knowing that I should have to carry out some foolish obligation—and that the consciousness of this obligation would remain with me forever.

True enough, I often rebel and try to convince myself of the opposite: it was Zina who came to me, while I promised nothing and declared in all honesty that I was not in love with her; she would do well to remember the brevity and ambiguity of our meetings, her rebuffs for any effusiveness, but still I cannot shake off a certain feeling of guilt and disappointment with myself. I never ring Zina up; very rarely, and always without forewarning, she will show up at my *pension*—as that playful Parisian expression goes, "*de cinq à sept*"—and find me wearily lounging around during these would-be reclusive hours; and each of our rapprochements is so like the first: every bit as unexpected and just as fraught with nerves. But I have no use for these meetings of ours—however infrequent, bewildering, or exhilarating they may be: they rob me of my only sanctuary (even my nights are not always peaceful—Zina is reckless and knows how to get at me), and besides, my hands are pitifully tied at the Wilczewskis', where some muddled sense of duty persistently draws me—to the house, to Ida Ivanovna, to Zina. Eagerly I imagine my imminent split with Zina (every time she takes offense, every time she spoils for a fight), and in an instant I see how much calmer and easier things would be for me, how much more convenient—the orderly management of my own time, one woman, an absence of unmitigated pity and legitimate self-reproach. I reread these entries and am amazed at the change I see in myself, a change that is incomprehensible yet seemingly not accidental—that I choose my business affairs, my women, practically even my own moods—yet it would appear that I am right only superficially; deep down, nothing has changed:

by no means have I chosen my present identity (buried as it is under layers of women, books, and cafés): this current identity is but the resurrection of my old deathly solitude, and I must turn to Zina (sometimes irritated, in a frenzy of humility) in order to recreate—in reverse order—those sweet days of Lyolya, days that briefly destroyed that deathly abandonment. I found being with Lyolya so captivating (I cannot find a better word for it) that even now I try, despite myself, to rediscover that old steady flame in Zina's feelings for me, to find Lyolya's aloofness and displeasure in the way that Zina irritates me, and lo, my extravagant, pointed betrayals with Ida Ivanovna, Zina's suspicions and rightful jealousy, my obligatory heartlessness fill me—for her sake, for that of the man I used to be before Lyolya, before the possibility of Lyolya's "betrayals"—with an unpleasant and uncommonly exhilarating pain that is every bit like the real thing. This intrusion of a pain connecting two of my extremes—how I have suffered and how I cause others to suffer—leads to a certain reconciliation with my fate and my own (until now seemingly unique and uniquely undeserved) failures far more clearly than any speculative, wholly unconvincing comparisons: since I now have that same dark, unnecessarily hurtful power over someone that Lyolya once had over me, that same nagging cruelty (born of animus), since I, sensible to and mindful of the wrong done to me, am capable of and even compelled to inflict it in turn, there is, one might even say, an inevitability to all this, an eternal exchange of roles that brings us hope and comfort on bad days. It was something odd and barely noticeable that made me think of my excessive and inevitable cruelty yesterday at the Wilczewskis': they were talking about a French novel, a recent *succès de scandale*, one much too risqué and close to the bone, and Zina, with comic directness, came over to me at once (I was sitting by the little table adorned with fruit) and, resting her hand on my shoulder, slightly crouching on her long legs, reached over me to the apples—she spent an indelicately long time selecting one and suddenly looked me in the eyes so expressively and shamelessly that I could actually feel her burning, involuntary abandon, a reluctance to control herself or obey my whims, a question so indignant and so understandable that my usual, somewhat mocking, judgmental disdain for Zina vanished in an instant. I ought to have quietly said, "I must see you later," or for all to hear—to calm and reassure—"What a marvelous evening. Why don't you see the guests off, and I'll bring you back later" (it would have been simple and, in that moment, perfectly justifiable on account of our mutual desire); but one obstacle yet remained—one that was irremediable, idiotic, tedious—and that was Ida Ivanovna, in whose presence not only could I not promise or suggest anything to Zina, but with whom I had, as it were, tacitly agreed to deceive Zina that very night. In the event, I said nothing and, annoyed with myself, projected my annoyance onto both women, while Zina, biting her lip theatrically, but sincerely perplexed and shocked, tapped her nail on the top apple and clumsily extricated herself from me. With some surprise, I thought how distressing it is to recognize in everything the inequality that we have wrought (even when it is in my favor): because of Ida Ivanovna, I have somebody with whom to ward off the dangerous sensuality that bedevils so many as yet unestablished relationships; Zina, on the other hand, has no one, and that is why she forever has this excessive readiness to abase herself and to surrender to me, to suffer these habitual disappointments. Because of other similar instances of my rudeness, ruthlessness, or simply my contrived, evasive blindness, I have begun to pardon—gradually coaxing them out of my memory—other moments of Lyolya's annoyance, her rash words, her stubborn refusal to see that I needed to be comforted, and how easy it would have been to give that comfort; and so, next to me, Lyolya appears almost heroic in her patience and condescension: indeed, to me, at least, it felt tormentingly sweet (because of the assurance of continual meetings, which assurance Zina lacks after my evasive blindness) to endure all that vitriol—because it was alive, because it was Lyolya's—vitriol that I did not attempt to avoid and at times even seemed to provoke. The inevitability of her growing bored with me back then is becoming ever clearer to me, but I believe that it would be a different story now: I know that Lyolya's boredom was caused by my eternal muddled attempts to foist my love on her, a love that was as unbearable as it was unrequited, but we had other things, too—the exchange of observations, jokes, ideals (which could be united under the term "friendship," and which was all that Lyolya found worthwhile and interesting in her conversations with me)—all this I would hide whenever I divined in her words an irritated haste in response to the loving tone of my own ones, sensible and inconsequential though they were. It pained Lyolya that I was oblivious to the real subject of our friendly conversations, that I understood nothing and did not make the likely futile efforts that in the future I shall make without fail and that will alter our complicated relationship, tainted as it has been by thoughtlessness. It is possible, of course, that even then I shall not be able to stand my ground and that, as usual, some rival will appear, attended by jealousy, striking at all human resoluteness; but I daresay that after Sergei N., Lyolya will be even more broken than before, even more in need of some calm and carefree respite.

Once again I am convinced that this change in myself (especially if it is not imaginary or deliberate, but arisen from genuine personal experience) is in some way a lesson in patience, fairness, and kindness, but this is not the first time that I have tried to apply this theoretical method (likely borrowed from somewhere), and its past success has depended on my being little hurt, whereas in the most wounding of circumstances—during spells of rivalry and jealousy, for instance, as I have just described—no decision holds fast, and the impossibility of achieving, predetermining, calculating, plunges us back into the unknown, into a struggle with only our helpless, already-defeated intuition to guide us—but then, just maybe, it also imbues our life with a bit of hope and the unconceited sense of dignity that would not exist, were it not for such failures—or, for that matter, the torments of the unknown.

In these half-hearted times (without submitting to daily duties imposed by all manner of little responsibilities, without blindly submitting to love), all the more soberly do I perceive the frailties and dangers posed by submission in its variety of forms—that fatal shortcoming in all our lives—and somehow I am able to compare them, and perhaps it is what remains of love, strangled yet still ennobling, that reveals to me just how much trivia there is in my cold, dull depths, in all the "weight" that I have finally achieved, and what remains compels me once again—albeit with something of an ulterior motive—not to be callous or indifferent, but to be conscientious, and to suffer.

July 7

T ODAY I RECEIVED an unexpected letter from Katerina Viktorovna: Lyolya has gone to Berlin for a few days with Sergei N. and asked her to send me that old photograph of her with clasped hands, the one that I myself would often remind her of; at the same time, emboldened and availing herself of the opportunity afforded by Lyolya's absence, Katerina Viktorovna has informed me of everything that she managed to glean over time, discussing Lyolya in that conspiratorial tone of devotion and with such a passionate attention to even the most trifling of details, and to their constant interpretation, which admits of no reproach and can only merit an indulgent, affectionate grin or a delightedly scandalized whisper, in a tone somewhat slavish and imbued with somebody else's life, the one in which old aunties will speak of a favorite, spoiled nephew, or faithful courtiers of their sovereign. The letter, of course, brought news of Lyolya's predicament: "Sergei Nikolayevich is a marvelous man and loves Lyolya enormously, but he does not know how to handle her." (It struck me that Katerina Viktorovna has not yet clocked how poorly I myself "handled" her.) "He has a difficult character, is quick to take offense, and won't say anything for days on end if Lyolya dares to contradict him, but you know what the girl is like, how frank and direct she can be. Besides, he is unspeakably jealous and scarcely bothers to conceal his jealousy." This was the sole criticism in the letter, a hint at something of which I was not aware, but it was immediately followed by more cheering words: "We talk about you all the time, and Lyolya insists that you alone were always able to cheer her up." I am beginning to believe it myself—over the six months of our "friendship," a great many things happened, and I am able to call to mind anything I like, some chance joke of mine that was especially successful, Lyolya's cheerful and approving laugh. That especially cunning, quick-witted laughter of hers, revived now in my memory, this lovely letter from Katerina Viktorovna—it has all of a sudden broken Lyolya's distance and unattainability and has revealed her to me anew, near to me, preoccupied with me: I smiled as it dawned on me just why she had sent me that photograph—Lyolya, sensitive, kind, apt not to forget the little things in the days when she was well-disposed toward me, had now thought of my potential anxiety, of my suspicions owing to her trip with Sergei N., and so from there, from afar, she seemed to nod at me reassuringly. Enchanted, I looked at the photograph of Lyolya, as though at something rare and precious, although I had seen this photograph only in Berlin—at Katerina Viktorovna's—and never in Lyolya's possession, and although I experienced after Berlin another feeling, the very same that brightened my recent boredom and was destroyed so entirely by Lyolya's overwhelming arrival. Ever since that arrival, however, I have always thought back on my first years in Paris, and those before them in Berlin, with a kind of wonder—they are touchingly and tenderly connected for me, now, with Lyolya, who at the time was only a name, while the other feelings that so suffused me back then seem cheapened, a dreary list of events, expectations, and developments that affect me now only if they are associated with Lyolya. Plainly, those whom we love at any given moment appear poeticized and near to us even in the memories that predate that love (if such memories in any way concern the object of our affection), while those whom we have ceased to love, whom we have replaced—at very least, for the duration of the replacement—seem dull and unpoetic not only now, but even in our romantic past, which is cast in a light (despite the truth of the matter in our heads) determined not by how we felt then, but by how we feel now. The photograph, the discussions about Lyolya in Berlin—they are all more acute than her suddenly revived but nevertheless pale laughter; they have unexpectedly drawn me to her and made me wish—ardently, capriciously, willfully—for her greater obtainability in some way, for some real, tangible embodiment, and I began impatiently to search, to pick over my—alas, limited—options: a letter was a tried and tested pleasure, but it entailed a less-than-immediate response; I could have tried asking Bobby and Zina, though I recalled their previous stories about Lyolya, which struck me simply for their mediocrity. What did that leave me with? Derval?

I could not put off a meeting; no sooner had I considered the prospect than I found myself racing there in a taxicab, astonished by both my extravagance and the groundlessness of my hopes, yet there was, as I soon discovered, a certain logic and meaning in this seemingly absurd and rash act. Derval, bored in the midst of work, forever ready to be distracted, beamed at me in delight—he loves these strange talks with me (about the revolution in Russia, about my supposed courting), and so, as if deciphering my intentions, having enquired for appearances' sake and for that of my shattered dignity about some routine affairs, he suddenly, with that same tension in his eyes and forehead with which he asks about matters of business, as though having recollected something of significance to us both, said to me quite naturally: *"Et votre amie, qu'est-ce qu'elle est devenue?"*

After several persistent questions, he formulated an accurate impression of the situation and, I thought, almost with a rival's sense of satisfaction, one understandable in an old man who has, at one time or another, been much loved, he sympathized with me and began to console me, saying that Lyolya would yet come back "to us" and that now "we" knew what the matter was and should not let her go. Such exceeding responsiveness to my earlier hopes (to have a chat about Lyolya; to listen, as it were, to the oracle; to have, as it were, my fortune told) even galled me a little—for this was yet another proof of that human omniscience, the insight of others that belittles mine; I was, essentially, comforted by the talk, and if by "gentlemanly" habit I preferred to remain silent, still I smiled intelligently enough. I daresay that Derval misinterpreted my silence, believing that he had gone too far in breaking the rules of decorum, and he cooled obdurately, as he had done previously after instances of incautious, bothersome chatter.

My presentiment about this visit to Derval was, I repeat, not in the least bit irrational: the revival of the past, the accuracy and intensity of the remembrance, depend in some measure on its enchanting fortuitousness; they appear a miracle, the gift of which has suddenly befallen us, and none of our artificial efforts can so resurrect the past anew, while every repeated attempt at revival—always somewhat artificial—will inevitably be feebler than the archetype (today's example: the unexpected receipt of the photograph, the unanticipated letter from Katerina Viktorovna but not one from Lyolya herself—her letters have become commonplace and scarcely excite me now), and if one were to try to find a way to revive the past, or to keep it revived, one would have to turn, just as I turned to Derval, to people and opportunities yet untried.

In fact, the miracle that was Lyolya's would-be presence today was maintained and strengthened at Derval's, not by his encouraging words, but by a single astonishing detail that almost escaped me at first, but later, all day long, seemed connected to Lyolya and to something about her that was, as far as I was concerned, reassuringly sweet and dear: she has an amusing knack for catching other people's expressions, their turns of phrase, even their intonations, and can mimic them with such infectious precision that they become a model of imitation, one that is understood by everybody and is inseparable from the person being imitated, and so today, thanks to Derval, I was reminded how Lyolya would make fun of him and recalled, as it were, her "imitation of an imitation." It is true—how we used to laugh and poke fun at that "old boy," repeating certain beloved phrases of his (*"mon cher, voilà"*), emulating that captain of industry's clipped, imperious, theatrical tone before any vital declaration (although it must be said that his imperious solemnity never lasts), and those curious, chesty, affectionate little notes intended to convince you of his friendship or of the benefit of some deal with a particularly useful individual. With his voice, Derval reminded me—in a strange and perverse fashion—of Lyolya and how she used to poke fun at him, reminded me with a freshness that was so sweet, so unexpectedly joyful, just like old times, that the feeling lasted all day long: to see Lyolya then and there, feigning seriousness, pleased by my laughter and already laughing with me, well-meaning, as she has so rarely been in these last few months, all I had to do was furrow my brow like Derval, look triumphantly ahead and say the magic words: *mon cher, voilà.*

Probably wishing to pin this down even more securely, I found myself, almost for the first time, reaching irresistibly for music—music is especially associated for some reason with romantic feelings, feelings that are, to some extent, replaced by it, that are intensified as it swells and mingles with them: both music and love entail that same ennobling dissociation from everything selfish and vain, that same fearless height. What pushed me in the way of music was a poster I happened to see for Tchaikovsky's "Pathétique" Symphony; I wanted to hear it immediately—as vindication for a joke that Lyolya made at my expense a long time ago. I am no judge of music; without somebody else's direction, I am hopelessly lost, and yet—although dependent, reliant on the verdict of others—I do love it, only I tire and will quickly begin to grow bored. I have heard the Sixth Symphony many times before and have read all manner of explanations that poeticize and inspire one's perception of it, and some of its independent spirit has trickled down to me: gone for me are its longueurs and novelty, forever so dangerously dispiriting, and I can relate to the now thoroughly familiar flow of sounds as I please. I hold the second and third movements to be things of perfection, even if they are a little shallow and frivolous, but then the first and final movements (it is possible that I am borrowing these words, but so lasting has been their impression) astonish me, like an echo of something that is, I daresay, deeply personal and terrifying. Fearing fatigue and boredom and, at the same time, the loss of Lyolya's appearance today, I decided to listen to nothing but the "Pathétique" Symphony, and truly it touched and uplifted me, as Lyolya's presence had never done, even when it was unexpected, well-intentioned, felicitous. Never have I ceased to know—clairvoyantly, deep down—that Lyolya is with me, or that she will be with me yet, that we are fated to be together, that one day, just as surely as I am listening to this symphony now, I shall explain it all to Lyolya, and she will come (through this musical connection) to understand that our friendship is in fact kinship. It strikes me that the only salvation from how I imagine—with terror and despair—man's station and his fate is to be found in Lyolya's succor. Like everyone, I have my own, maybe obsessive, futile, maybe in some way authentic, vision: all of a sudden, I will imagine the entire homogenous world as it is

revealed to us—the streets, the cities, the rooms, those intelligent beasts of a sad and predatory nature, who have learned
to stand on their hind legs, who have built all this but are
fated to disappear, who, despite this, still try to cling to something solid and lasting, still try to ward off the inevitability of
death, who dreamed up fairy tales and, now that these stories
have been disproved, are disconsolate—and for me the only
means of defending myself from our terrible fate is love, my
love—Lyolya. Without love we fall into a stupor or despair, it
covers our naked animal essence; with the fear of death, with
deliberate attempts to grab hold of some kind of eternity, one
that is at once a mystery to us and yet devised by us, even the
remains of love, even its very echo in music, imbues us with
a semblance of fearlessness, dignity, and the spiritual range
to disregard death. Only by loving, by knowing about love,
hoping for love, are we inspired and meaningfully engaged
in life, able to banish the sovereignty of petty day-to-day
cares, to stop waiting for the end to come; hence my conclusion, my hope—despite all doubt, despite experience, despite
my perennial, easily pacified patience: Lyolya must love—
for my sake (thankfully I have mellowed, and it startles me to
think for the first time—for her own sake, too); she cannot
leave me, else she will know how feeble, how inadequate and
elusive are the remains of love, and how, before we realize it,
it will be too late. Because of the enormous triple strain—
Lyolya's almost tangible presence all day, somebody else's
dying, desperate music, my own foolish fever—I have ceased

to doubt and now begin to believe, with rejoicing, with relief, that Lyolya has already staged her intervention.

MY FOOLISH FEVER continues yet: urged on by obsessive nocturnal observations, I have had to jump out of bed and now I race to inscribe my thoughts in pencil, and in all likelihood tomorrow I shall regret what I have written—for in the morning it always proves worthless and of dubious significance—but still I cannot help myself. The first such observation: the terrific heat forced me to lie down on top of the duvet and inadvertently I felt—one on top of the other— the warmth of my legs, and suddenly I recalled how last winter at Lyolya's I undressed in the dark, how embarrassed I was by my ice-cold legs, rubbing them for so long and fearing to touch Lyolya, and now it pains me to realize that the night is passing, and so with it all this wasted, living warmth meant for Lyolya. I felt something vaguely like this when I was a child, when the dog, loved and doted on by all our family, ran off one day during a walk, after which at each and every meal I would feel sad—with a touch of that same mercenariness that I now foster for what is untouched—that bones and titbits intended for our beloved pet were going to waste, no longer of use to anybody.

No, my observations began with something else: when I entered my room, I saw on the table a bar of chocolate in its wrapper—ordinarily, this would have brought a sense a comfort, prosperity, "everything in its rightful place," hope amid all this loneliness, but today it symbolized something more, something so shameful that I am loath to write about it. Nor indeed shall I write about it: I do not mean to dramatize, but, simply put, I am already quite certain that I shall boldly cross out these rather wet, debasing, self-pitying words that only mar these pages granting Lyolya resurrection, pages that are particularly pleasing to reread.

PART III

THE TRAIN WAS late, and Lyolya, brushing her cheek against my chin (the touch of it was indescribably fresh and tender), began to tell me with great animation how the train had been stopped right outside the station and how all the passengers had been made to show their papers (clearly, they were looking for some fugitive criminal), how pleasant and easy the journey had been, how at night a man—in an attempt to flirt with her—had offered up the seat next to him, after which she had got some rest and slept "better, more comfortably than at home": why is it that people who have not seen each other in a long while, having prepared themselves to listen and talk about everything under the sun, everything remarkable, important, and new that has happened to each of them, suddenly immerse themselves in idle, meaningless chatter about whatever has gone on immediately before their encounter? Perhaps it is the accidental, the inconsequential, that is simply more alive in our memory than anything else, anything old and important, which we so rarely recall even in ordinary, mundane, more humdrum times, not broken by long separations; still more likely is that we unconsciously strive to adjust ourselves to the most recent circumstances of our newly encountered friend, while just as unconsciously we reattune the friend to ourselves. And sure enough, soon after those first meaningless words and joint struggles with her luggage, in the taxi as we approached her new and more expensive hotel, Lyolya, as if only just having found me, suddenly said with conviction and emotion:

"Really, you are such a dear."

I was immediately put at ease by this: Lyolya was with me, and for the time being I no longer had to fear her every word, her every smile, those long pauses, or to interpret everything, as I used to do, examining it from every angle—worrying that she was angry but hiding her irritation, or that she had calmed down, but only for a short while. That most blessed day of recompense seemed to be upon me, a reward bestowed simply for a period of friendship, for the agonies and ecstasies of some arbitrary length of time, for the good days and the bad that we had already shared, for the fact that I had spent months waiting for Lyolya faithfully, for the fact that we had both of us had our infidelities, for the fact that we now shared a respectable patchwork "history" that was uniquely our own. Much in this unaccustomed and sweet camaraderie of ours is connected, I find: pride in the past, in our easy mutual understanding, in our friendly equality, and another thing altogether—the neurasthenic's beloved sense of respite after something longed for and finally attained.

When a relationship like this has been established—one that demands thoughtfulness and a cool head, one that is truly calm and not exasperating—we accept more simply and benignly what in other circumstances would have piqued us and caused an argument: scarcely did I even notice Lyolya's admission about the money given to her by Sergei N. (he has gone off to shoot a film in America) or the elusive change in her that this sudden security has wrought—plans for the future, notions of business and travel, all expressed in a new tone of almost absolute certainty—without the least disapproval I accepted that Lyolya should feel no shame over Sergei N.'s generosity, and that she should be glad to be free of cares, delighted with tomorrow's expensive dresses, with this clean, almost-grand hotel. With a strange incoherence—perhaps on account of that typical bold candor of hers—Lyolya informed me, with a reassuring, encouraging smile, how terrible it had been with Sergei when finally it became clear that they just could not get along together, that they had to break up, and how Sergei—"after everything that's happened"—would of course never leave her "in poverty." Feeling no real, genuine sense of reproach, I hardly registered not only Lyolya's reckless promiscuity, but also my own squeamishness in that regard: after all, I was agreeing, in a certain sense, to take on somebody else's concern for Lyolya, to show the generosity of a man or, essentially, a lover. However, my swift consent to this cannot be explained by some self-serving sense of indolence (that I am myself in no way obliged to Lyolya, I admit freely; I have no need to put on airs now or to prove myself), I simply declined to dwell upon anything that fell beyond what was essentially obvious, beyond what had revealed itself to me little by little and now suddenly consumed me: namely, that Lyolya was at last in the same city as me and reachable at a moment's notice—for answers given in person, for hand-kissing or sweet, seemingly accidental contact, for the constant admiration of her voice, her choice of words, her complicity in my inner tension, everything about our hotly felt prox-imity. In one sense, I have changed—somehow instantly and unaccountably—in my ability to manage my internal work, to direct my indifferent daily efforts wherever and however I will: only yesterday I was able to arrange everything in whatever dazzling order I pleased (hence all my efficiency, a modicum of success, and an unaccustomed sense of ennui); how effortlessly I induced myself to daydream of Lyolya until such-and-such an hour (my eternal mode of rest and relax-ation), only then to prepare for a business meeting or, as proved hardest of all, to devise my evening pages, to wring out the words, to find their proper semantic and rhythmic order, whereas today I have been absorbed exhilaratingly in Lyolya's delightful presence, and to deny myself it—for the sake of anything else—would be unnatural and pointless form of self-injury.

Occasionally I will try to understand the nature of such unabashed, all-consuming obsession as I have now. Many attempts to explain it (putting it down to attraction, inevitable conflict, fear of loss) speak only of the trigger, of what can cause, underpin, or intensify obsessions such as ours, while its essence, its soul, so to speak, lies elsewhere: a woman with whom we are so inordinately, so trustingly preoccupied becomes invisible, unaware of her role as the arbiter of our actions, our conversations, even our secret, never-to-be-divulged decisions, and we blindly adopt her views (regardless whether genuine or merely attributed to her by us), or rather her tastes—whatever she approves of or praises with unconscious conviction—and we alter our own views and tastes in line with hers and even single-mindedly alter ourselves, for we need unconditional, unbroken, minute-by-minute approval, and, like savages before our own god, we will continually (and, of course, mentally) ask a woman who has reluctantly conquered our hearts about every littlest, most inconsequential thing, making her imperceptibly into a kind of semi-abstraction of our conscience, and hence our romantic obsession is inspired and enlivened by a special, heightened consciousness (as in its naïve awareness is the body by the soul), one that makes us uncommonly demanding of ourselves, and so we needs must have a clear and unblemished conscience—for the stronger and keener the original cause and stimulus of such obsession, whatever it may be (obscurity, fear of loss, conflict—alone or in combination, all at once), the more we need that approval. And now, having fallen on words about this astonishing romantic conscience that metamorphoses simply into conscience, I once again come up against an assumption that is, for any religious person, arbitrary and blasphemous, an assumption about the possibility of replacing something otherworldly and supposedly irreplaceable with a local, all-pervading, human love.

All this unusually high-flown emotion of mine seems to depend somewhat on a certain depth in the relationship that has now taken shape between me and Lyolya—I desire nothing for myself, nor do I ask questions or make accusations (which I have so long and spitefully prepared), and it feels both strange and easy to remain indifferent, incurious, and patient. The blissful clarity of that first day was interrupted quite unexpectedly. We were sitting together in a café from which Lyolya, conscientious and punctual as ever, was expected to make a telephone call on the instruction of some Berlin acquaintance. When she got up, I looked at her with mock entreaty, as though begging her to allow me to accompany her to the telephone and not to be left alone—previously, such "unnecessary things" were not allowed, but now that the relationship is less obtrusive, "without strings," and has a friendly air about it, Lyolya can no longer quibble with every one of my apparently romantic demands, and, with a laugh, she indicated her approval with a nod. We found ourselves—as though in sequestration—in a tiny, dark booth; I offered to connect Lyolya with the number she required and occupied myself with the tedious task, after which, having succeeded, at liberty now, I suddenly saw her glowing tenderly in the dark, right there beside me—practically up against me and within terrifying reach—and I was struck by that mysterious, gnawing fear that reawakens everything we once held dear and then suppressed or else cravenly set aside for an indefinite period of time, and so what I had suppressed once again came to life—the sweetness of our embrace, the possibility that we should never be parted, loyalty, the hope of coming to some lasting arrangement with her, a kind of hard-won sanctity for my mortal love. It seemed simply ridiculous not to caress Lyolya, not to touch her with my hand, not to kiss her, and the melodious sound of her low-pitched voice seemed to pour forth just for me, and it was deeper, more imbued with meaning than those impersonally polite phrases that she had to shout down the telephone. My patience reached its end. Lyolya intuited this immediately and, without making a single movement—amid the uninterrupted flow of the telephone conversation—somehow brought me down to earth with her disappointment and dissatisfaction. My half-forgotten state of rejection, bitterness, and pain returned to me at once, and I simply marveled at the precision of the coincidence—how closely had two so asynchronous states of mine coincided, two feelings of resentment, the former already forgotten, and the latter novel and acute—as if I had been liberated from a suffocating chloroform mask, only for the mask to be replaced again after a few minutes of sweet fresh air. Such precision of coincidence never happens in verbal communication, in the dutiful, deliberate act of remembering, and this fact has mystified me numerous times already: I keep returning to the same thing, tying myself in knots and never quite managing to disentangle myself—why should it be that the artificial reconstruction of the past (provided that it is both diligent and conscientious) is so often stronger, sharper than what we try to reconstitute ourselves—even if it is forever distinct? We can create something that has never been, that resembles what has been and yet is more than what it was, something palatable to our discriminating, pampered consciousness, but we shall never recreate what has been, while nature occasionally returns the past to us in all its charming and impermanent bloom. Observing this staggering difference—between this accidental, intrusive recreation and our own attempts to imitate it—I find myself contemplating a river of eternity flowing toward us but never away from us, thinking that what is created by us is unique, inimitable, exceptional, and yet it will never be eternal—hence its poignancy, its isolation from dull life the whole world round, and hence its heroic futility.

I had to take significant pains so that all this, at first confusing, series of thoughts that sparked from so minor an incident—fleeting fear in a telephone booth—but seemed so important, so that all this could be set aside until evening, so that later, as I walked home from Lyolya's, I could recall everything, contrive to organize my thoughts, and, late that night—right now, in fact—set them down in writing, habituating myself (if only in some small way) to that mental discipline that in Lyolya's absence—because of poverty, a dearth of temptations and distractions—had come so easily, that is now almost impossible, but without which there can be no creativity. There is still a kind of resistance in me—the remnant of prolonged indifference and dull obduracy—and this befits my current restraint and incuriosity regarding Lyolya: this is why I have quickly and painlessly overcome a dangerous rush of hope and an even more dangerous feeling of bitterness brought on by detachment and disillusionment. But for that moment, the day passed rather monotonously, in a touching, amicable clarity that seemed to dispel the possibility of love's reciprocity, for which—clandestinely and with blithe confidence—I had been preparing myself more than anything. But then, such a possibility was always imaginary and so implausible after all my woeful experiences with Lyolya, which have only confirmed to me time and again that love cannot be forced. These exaggerated, inane hopes reappeared, I think, in Blainville, one of those salubrious holiday spots in Normandy; though a casino is under construction there and a fashionable resort is being planned, it is, for the moment, cheap and quiet, hence my having spent two restful weeks there at the end of summer. After long being habituated to the city, to the prospect of distraction each and every minute of the day (every crowd, every couple, every young woman in a café, in the street and on the Métro fascinates me), after my unjustified scorn for any foreign, hopelessly alien nature, those weeks in Blainville proved simply and unexpectedly enchanting. I wound up there quite by chance, on the advice of an acquaintance, and, excited, uplifted by my first bit of good luck—that I had managed to install myself in a pleasant and well-appointed *pension*—I set out at once for a stroll, taking a childish, unspoiled pleasure in the unfamiliar wonders of a country walk: the recent rain and the glinting, not yet importunate sun, had imbued the air with a lively sense of exultation, of lightly sparkling droplets (like tears of joy after irrepressible, rollicking laughter), the exultation of exhaustion, freshness, and purity—for some reason it put me in mind of great, thirsty gulps of sharp-tasting spring water. I followed the unpaved, muddy road, stepping cheerfully on the bona-fide naked earth (and regretting only my shoes, which were rustified and mud-spattered), and suddenly I was struck by the vague recognition of something that once belonged to me, something distant, long forced out by time, feelings, and events. I wanted to be alone, to see no one, lest the locals interfere with the return of my past, with my as yet unestablished concentration—I hurried past the last building on the road, the empty, unfinished casino, past the silent, hostile-looking workers in their soiled white shirts (the casino was to the left, while to the right there was a pale little lake, from which a fine layer of water came rushing over the uneven ground, creating turbid, slippery little impromptu waterfalls that rumbled and trembled like aspic); after that point I encountered nobody else, and before long I found myself in a long, dark alley that was lined on both sides with a neat row of trees, placed so close together that they formed a continuous, lofty canopy. For some while, I had felt as though at any moment I could enter a cave or a barn, one that was dangerous and completely isolated—truly, it was all so deserted, frightening, and damp, just like a dungeon—but the solitude, the invigorating chill in the air and the absence of people (forever judging and getting in the way) helped to foster a sense of elation, one that had begun earlier and demanded immediate action, a fierce and conquering will. To my right, the waterfall's yellowish foam babbled and gurgled as it was borne away, while to the left of the alley a patch of woodland rose steeply (it was small, but so wild and overgrown, so dense that one could conceivably lose one's way in it)—I walked along the echoing, solid earth (likely, the rain had not penetrated here because of the leaves), past roots that reminded me of springboards in a gymnasium, and more and more I wanted to take a run and jump, deftly, powerfully, and go flying off into the distance. I began to climb the steep, difficult embankment, breaking off branches and leaves, scattering sand, kicking up—as though they were balls— clumps of hardened, dried-out moss, and somehow I managed to convince myself, cheerfully, drunkenly, passionately, that nothing was beyond my reach. Like Tchaikovsky's symphony, the impersonal, solitary grandeur of the place remade me in its own image, ennobled me, made me hope that Lyolya would understand, believe that she could not fail to grasp the unselfishness of my devotion, my readiness to enrich her and never to ask anything in return, that all she need do was make her way to that marvelous, revelatory place, and that I, with all the stubbornness that I had accrued there, would be able to bring her, by force if necessary, and surround her with all that friendly, foolproof scenery. But then, as I led Lyolya there in my mind, I forgot about the unselfishness of my devotion and began to take charge of Lyolya's fate much too expediently for my liking: what seemed so attainable was the very miracle of not being parted, which, as far as I could see, was possible only in marriage (the commonplace naïveté of an aging bachelor), and I imagined, or rather, no, I did not hesitate to believe, that our correct and tender family life was in some way guaranteed—in gentle companionship throughout work and rest, in agreeable, amenable, as it were, harmonious conversations, in a dignified, rarely expressed love, with well-earned trust and implicit freedom, with the bedroom door on a lock (so as to shut out the world), with occasional strolls through this very alley, reverently renewing our manifest love. With quick steps (as though driven on by my overheated, overjoyed imagination) I left the alley and made my way back toward the lake. Not far from it, on a lawn at the bottom of a hill, there was a modest country café—round tables on thick wooden legs, folding chairs, a tiny building in the middle where everything was laid out and prepared—but, as in a genuine "tea-room," there were starched girls in caps running deftly about the lawn with trays and people lounging about who seemed so out of place after the wildness and solitude of the past hour that I had spent—now I delighted in them, as new sources of inspiration, as witnesses of hope and recently sprung immense joy, and so I ensconced myself among them, kindly, almost ingratiatingly observing, sympathizing even with the ones I assumed to be enamored young couples;

together with them, I reveled in the charm of the light breeze blowing from the lake, my face turned to it, my eyes closed, sharing my pleasure also with Lyolya, and I was taken unawares when the time eventually came to reckon with the late hour: I suddenly imagined that I was paying for Lyolya, taking care of her, that she was pleased with the day, complimenting me and proud of me. In the evening, in my rather narrow but cozy room, along with the books that I had brought with me, along with the chaste, somewhat too-firm bed, along with the walls that let through, that broadcast any and every noise, I—owing to my faith in Lyolya's long-standing, time-honored, head-spinning proximity—might well have thrown open the door and come face-to-face with her, as though after many years of marriage, devoid of any importunate passion, as though I were meeting a faithful, reliable, never-deceitful friend. Secretly, hiding behind the fact that I knew of its fictiveness, I held this prospect of love's reciprocity, fidelity, marriage—the most precious and touching thing that Blainville had to offer—at arm's length, fueling it all the while, but when Lyolya eventually arrived back in Paris, eliciting from me a new, wary, defensive sense of restraint, this prospect instantly vanished, far too immaterial as it was, having been born not of reality, but of some ethereal conditions (lofty though they were) inspired by music or nature, and having crumbled at the first touch of real life, at the first words I heard spoken on Lyolya's living lips, and, when I tried to insist on the trip (my reason, as usual, lagging a little behind), my attempts at persuasion seemed to lack conviction and even the secret knowledge that I was right.

In checking my initial, irrational élan, I lost that heroic blindness that occasionally leads us to utterly irreparable consequences and found myself in my usual state of wariness, circumspection, and fearful calculations—how to handle money, how to get enough of it for two, would it not be better to stop agonizing so much and not to alter anything: it was as if I had been forced to give up everything that I had once held to be my own—reciprocated love, a robust and long-lived happiness—but then, if all of this had in fact come about, I should have been immediately wracked by fear of penury, by my responsibility to Lyolya, by the inadequacies of what I had done for her, and these many cruel fears, this constant insatiable struggle, would have surpassed and supplanted my love.

It often seems to me that I have been cast into this world helpless and unwanted; any bit of luck, particularly in matters of money, will seem accidental, the last of its kind, and if the money begins to dry up, I prefer to wring myself out to the point of poverty, to the most disgraceful destitution, until the incomprehensible miracle of money appears yet another "last" time—and to live so precariously, all the while having to think about Lyolya too, about her pitiful dependence on this haphazard way of life, is simply unbearable; I have neither the courage for it, nor, in all likelihood, the shamelessness. Besides, I know by habitual, quickly humbling instinct, developed over the course of many defeats, that Lyolya, no matter how tender or sweet she may be with me, will leave me, give our reciprocity the slip, that in degrees, in the fullness of joy, I have my limits—and this prudence in matters of love coincides with my prudence in life itself.

Nevertheless, a certain circumspection was also apparent in the way in which I prepared to meet Lyolya, and, before her arrival, like a bridegroom or a husband, I tried to disentangle myself from those "frayed threads of bachelorhood"—or rather, it was not so much the circumspection as it was the straightforward obstinacy of a maniac, one who gets his own way and, blind to the wrong he has done, carries on removing one obstacle after another. Granted, my "liberation from the threads of bachelorhood"—from Ida Ivanovna and from poor Zina who has recently taken ill—was no mere detail among the many others that heralded and paved the way for Lyolya's arrival, but something pleasing in its own right: I had, long before, brutely decided to deliver myself from both women; all I lacked was the impetus to see through these latest excruciating explanations. Having since found that impetus, however—in the fact of Lyolya's arrival—these explanations have at last taken place, and what is more, they proved to be cruel, cold, almost businesslike.

It was easier, of course, to get rid of Ida Ivanovna: I braced myself, knowing full well that I should have to spend ten agonizing minutes, minutes that would be forgotten instantly and after which I would return to my pleasant thoughts about

Lyolya. For a solitary moment, there was even a temptation—from some calculating and apparently deep-rooted instinct of mine—not to leave Ida Ivanovna, to dodge those ten minutes of agony. Lyolya would never learn of my secret "affair," while the affair itself would be unwittingly translated into a counterbalance, a cynical mode of self-defense, one that was previously lacking yet is so necessary in unequal relationships, in such cases as my helplessness before Lyolya's feminine wiles. But so often my head—because of the examples that I have long tried to emulate, because of my own worthy deeds and the tender feeling of pride that I nurture on their account—proves nobler than my true nature, and it was in this mind that I resolved to be pure of intention and uncalculating with respect to Lyolya, to have it tediously out with Ida Ivanovna and, even though it would have been far more convenient, not to send her a letter ending things, one that was slighting through and through and, as it were, put paid to her. The nobility in my head is also expressed in the fact that I am tacitly (within the limits of "gentlemanliness") frank with both women and do not contest assertions that I am in love not with either of them, but with Lyolya. On the basis of this well-established and unaffected spirit of utmost candor, I decided simply to inform Ida Ivanovna of Lyolya's imminent arrival, certain of the impression that this information would make and leaving her to draw and articulate her own conclusions. In the event, when I carried out my decision, I saw once again just how skillfully Ida Ivanovna can make herself inconspicuous, unobtrusive, and invisible, and how she could never demand the same of me.

"Yelena Vladimirovna will be arriving any day now, you know."

"I thought she might. So, you won't be coming anymore?" (Then, after my affirmative silence.) "There's nothing worth saying. We'll say good-bye—and that will be the end of it."

"You're right, of course—as always."

I was delighted by her laconic, masculine grit. In fact, she seemed less bewildered than usual: perhaps this was her role in life—to endure the insults, the slights, the scorn from whomever she was seeing. Or, likelier still, she was simply indifferent to me and needed me (as she would have done any other) for nothing more than to "divert her sensuality."

Having it out with Zina was a far more difficult affair, since she was, quite evidently, in love with me, although she aroused in me (slightly spoiled though I am) only a combination of irritation and pity—even when she is out of sight and I recall her pale, downcast face preparing itself for a humiliating rebuff, I find myself annoyed at both myself and fate, that it is Zina—unpretentious, helpless Zina—whom I insult and torment, alone or in front of everybody; whenever she pays me a visit, and especially when she takes an age, an eternity, to leave, I can scarcely master myself enough to conceal my impatience, to avoid speaking a truth that she has long already known. Seemingly for the first time in all our acquaintance (and now—oh, the irony—so that we should go our separate ways), I asked her, of my own accord, to meet me in a café. I began as I did with Ida Ivanovna, with the news of Lyolya's arrival, but Zina—whether out of discretion or pride—never said in so many words what she would have been within her rights to think, and what she complained of nevertheless faintly and confusingly. In that moment, she did not betray herself, but only blushed dimly, while her eyes glittered indignantly.

"You will not see Yelena Vladimirovna. The doctor X-rayed me today. I'm very, very ill and I'm going away to Switzerland with Papa. You must come and be with me."

"But I can't right now—and not at all because of Yelena Vladimirovna."

"You mean your business affairs, finances. Oh, please . . . That's a fiction. Anything is possible if you truly put your mind to it."

I had the intolerable, hateful urge (because of this encroachment on my freedom) to get up, walk out, and never to see Zina again, and this forced me—contrary to my usual persuasive *délicatesse* in such circumstances—to declare rudely and indignantly:

"I will not be going."

Zina looked at me with unexpected tenderness, as though she were rephrasing the question, as though she were giving me time to reconsider and to comprehend in full the merciless cruelty of my refusal, but without so much as a word—with only a perplexed gesture of my hand and a shrug—I communicated that there was nothing to reconsider. Then, with a passionate reproach that reminded me of our first intimacy and my lengthy subsequent repentance, she said solemnly, almost theatrically:

"You're committing a murder."

I paused to think for a moment—such an evocative phrase, fit for the stage—but as I departed, having bid her farewell, having left her standing there motionless, as though unable to believe this final, definitive act of cruelty on my part, I felt as though I ought to have vindicated myself somehow, riled myself with honest, logical thoughts—that I had not sought Zina's love, that if at first she had allowed herself to think that I might reciprocate her feelings, then now she could no longer harbor any doubts (after all, I was never the first to call her, and never once had I forced myself to utter any obliging words of love, however tender or heartfelt)—but even if my reasoning was logical, sound, correct, still I could not shake off this feeling of agitation, and I experienced a lingering sense of treachery and dishonesty. As I walked along the street, delighting in the animation and warmth of summer, free now of the difficult task that I had set myself, experiencing the particular sweetness of security (not for all the world would I ever return to that café, never again would I see Zina or surrender myself to her reproaches, and now I could await Lyolya without impediment), I continued to take comfort in certain truths learned long ago—of the inadmissibility of encroaching on somebody else's freedom, of the need to hold one's own, of the shamelessness in coercing others or disregarding them—granted, all these easy truths, with which I now defended myself, I learned through experience that was inverse, remorseless, suicidal even, when it was I who was ashamed of my importunate and wholly unwarranted attempts to curtail somebody else's freedom, a fact from which I would often run. But even if I was right in my treatment of Zina and tried to act irreproachably in these situations, her injunction—"You will not see Yelena Vladimirovna"—remained lodged in my memory, so decisive (doubtless she had thought that was the way to handle people) and yet so defenseless, as did her bewilderment as I left the café and she cried out after me with such pitiful solemnity: "Murderer!" We often hold those we love to be accountable to us, and sometimes we simply cannot get away from the obviously absurd demands we make of them—recalling and knowing this (and precisely because I recalled and knew it), I could not get away from the opposite, from a feeling of responsibility to Zina, who loved me, from comparing her weakness to my strength, from the straightforward conclusion that I am in some way obliged to take care of her. It even seemed unfair to have forgotten about Ida Ivanovna altogether—only because she had said nothing, because the meek forever lose out—but it just so happened that this rivalry of the unloved was equalized naturally and easily: I loved another, a third, an outsider to them both—Lyolya—and the joy I felt for her immediately supplanted everything else. Calm reason, so cruel in poor Zina's case, yet so noble where Lyolya is concerned, has proved victorious—my only regret is that the heights I have reached with her will not last and will be broken by our forthcoming trip, by the excessive hopes that I place on this trip, hopes that will never be realized. This was the only failure of my reasoning today—as though I had unleashed some previously shackled desires and, having gone dashing after them, was unable to stop them in their tracks.

Keeping this diary has become easier for me—I have more words at my disposal, words ready to express something of my own, I have a greater variety of ways in which to combine them and I have developed the habit of summoning them at will; my observations are no longer exhausted at once, but rather they cling to one another, allowing me to extract everything about them that is new. I even fear this indefatigable ease, I deliberately linger over some difficult point and pedantically, stubbornly seek out elusive verbal solutions, solutions that seem the only true and exact ones; no artificiality can replace my natural inner efforts, however, and, having found the words I need, I carry on hastily writing these entries, as though in pursuit of everything that would otherwise be lost and forgotten: of course, diligent diaristic work, as with any other endeavor, will, with time and exertion, become a craft, a practice, and will no longer entail difficulty or novelty, the passion to conceal or to exalt what has been recorded with such enduring mystery. I cease now to think of the benevolent, loving woman who alone shall have the honor of reading and understanding—but no, I envisage the reader, indifferent, impartial, and, of course, I can foresee the disdainful perplexion: for in trying in good faith, without any duplicity, to depict something of my own, I end up, as it were, betraying myself—I will discover something bad therein, the things that people ordinarily hide (often even from themselves), and so, despite myself, I sometimes feel ashamed of what I achieve.

September 19

THERE IS A certain something that I have come to realize—concerning the imprudence, the folly of this trip to Blainville—and I feel no pride whatsoever on account of this realization; I have no vain, inner pretense. I simply have no time for all that—for the period prior to Lyolya's return seems to me an extraordinary, unique happiness, even if it did pass slowly, tediously, contemptibly. Right now, I find myself in that most hateful of conditions—an unending fit of jealousy—and my rival, unexpected as he is, is the unaccountably lucky Bobby Wilczewski, for whom, even as my rival, I foster little curiosity. It was I who suggested that Lyolya bring Bobby to Blainville, to ward off disappointment (our idyll could never have lasted) and the temptation of adjoining rooms, late-night strolls, and conversations: I had anticipated Lyolya's resistance and wanted to maintain a prudent, comfortable levelheadedness. Alas, however, there is much that I had not counted on—not only Lyolya's caprices and Bobby's ridiculous success, but also my own enduring thralldom to the nature at Blainville, to the dark tree-lined alley, to the hill with the café by the lake, to everything that they represented for me and for which I needed their help. Was there a hidden poison in all this nature, one that I encountered when I was alone here, or is it rather that my embellishments and exaggerations have infected my travelling companions and, by some strange, dubious logic, cast them together, fresh and new, while casting me aside, exhausted by all this? At any rate, I have missed my chance for a worthy friendship with Lyolya forever, lost all hope of winning and keeping her friendship, and I have forsaken that feeling of equilibrium that comes from contenting myself with that friendship. I am sick of people preferring another over me, sick of pride, sick of what is rudely, cruelly apparent, and the only thing that could now cure me is my own triumph, a clear sign of victory, the acceptance of far-fetched conditions— that Lyolya would settle down with me forever and never see or hear from Bobby again. How ridiculously at odds all this is with the true state of our relations, and unceasingly I hatch naïve and childish plans (both vengeful and placatory), forever telling myself how I shall disappear, how I shall leave Lyolya alone with Bobby, and how she, having lost me, with only Bobby to rely on, will be horrified and inevitably repent.

We arrived toward evening and were informed at the *pension* of our exceptional good luck (*"quelle veine vous avez"*)—that the casino was opening that very evening. I invited Lyolya to go for a stroll before dinner and to sit in the open air at the café, which back in Paris I had so rapturously and long-windedly described to her (praising it, as though it were my own), but Lyolya said that she preferred to rest and get herself ready. Bobby disappeared immediately, apparently to telephone his father, and so I set out alone down the familiar path. It was windy, cool, and damp—ahead of me, a discerning gentleman was revealing to his lady-friend the absurdity of opening a casino at the very end of the season. They, too, were heading in the direction of the café, and I—on account of some mischievous curiosity—took the table next to them. My curiosity was aroused by the lady, who was still quite young—pale, slender, and tall, like many a fashionable dancer—and, judging by her accent, undoubtedly Russian. She spoke little, however, and only in reply—distractedly, at that, and often missing the point entirely. Her companion, puce from all those aperitifs, a thickset and bald Frenchman with a graying moustache and a rosette bestowed by the Légion d'honneur, was trying to drag her into an absurd argument about Russia, attacking her rather ungraciously and showing off his formidable erudition and arguments: "*un peuple mérite le régime qu'il a, vous, les Russes—c'est Lénine ou bien Ivan le Terrible . . . voyez ceux qui entouraient ce pauvre tzar, ils l'ont tous abandonné, c'étaient tous des lâches, lâches, lâches.*" It is possible that he was just teasing her, or that this pale demoiselle, following the example set by so many émigré women, was for this foreigner "*du meilleur monde*" and, hence, "of the tzar's inner circle," in which case his insulting words were directed at her—at any rate, she was hardly listening, argued with him reluctantly and lackadaisically, and, unnoticed by him, exchanged several glances with me, lowering her limpid blue eyes, as it were, too expressively and revealing her protruding upper set of rather elongated teeth. I wanted to wade in on their argument, to startle her with the fact that I am Russian and on the same side, so to speak, and to charm him with my upstanding, sensible, winning objections. But I was almost out of time; I was drawn more to Lyolya, and I hadn't the strength to overcome unfamiliarity and the difficulty of taking that first step. On the way back, however, abuzz with unspent energy, I romantically imagined that poor Russian woman's financial dependence (and I doubt I was mistaken in this), how the wealthy Frenchman must "lord it over her," and how I would recount this exceptional, wistful, affecting observation, this slice of life, to Lyolya. Perhaps it was not quite so astonishing and unique as I had believed (I often exaggerate the things I save up for Lyolya—because of the enormity of the inspiring resonance that I find in her), or perhaps I simply failed to choose the right moment, but Lyolya heard me out with polite, insultingly contrived attention, nodding patiently (if only not to prolong the experience), only then to resume her conversation with Bobby, which I had interrupted—about the telephone, what news there was, and the health of his sister. I felt disproportionately piqued by this slight, for I had previously been so certain of the impression that the story would make, that it would hit the mark, that she would appreciate how it was packed with kindness, friendliness, nobility even. At the same time, my clumsy interference made me look like an outsider, surplus to Lyolya and Bobby's grown-up conversation, and this unbearable feeling carried on till the morning, becoming only more justified.

It suddenly struck me that I was quibbling, as so often I have done before, over minutiae, and that nothing, essentially, had changed—so as to test this, I convinced Lyolya (and, despite myself, out of politeness, Bobby too) to accompany me straight after dinner to that very same tree-lined alley, expecting once again to find there some much-needed friendly support. Lyolya agreed without any enthusiasm and only asked solicitously:

"Won't you be cold, Bobby dear?"

All the way, with uncustomary (for her) and in no wise ironic gentility, Lyolya kept harping on the same questions, while I, in my torment, wondered why she showed no care or solicitude for me, the mirror image of Bobby, although clearly less hardy and healthy, and I settled on what seemed to be the only conciliatory hypothesis possible—that Lyolya held me to blame for this frivolous stroll and so that was why she insisted on being so defiantly and unilaterally solicitous. We passed by the radiant, white, noisy casino, right on the lake— gusts of sharp, raw cold seemed to blow from it—and all of a sudden Lyolya cheered up:

"Here's what we'll do, Bob."

She deftly threw off her thick warm cardigan and placed its left sleeve over Bobby's left shoulder and the right one over her own—they had to clutch the cardigan firmly (each holding the end of one arm) and press close to each other—we found ourselves once again in a dark spot, where the two of them together (Bobby, big and broad, and Lyolya, smaller and narrower, sharing the cardigan, which hung at a slant from Bobby's shoulders down to Lyolya's) resembled some monstrous four-legged creature. I walked to the right of Lyolya, not touching her, making an offended show of my distance and alienation—of course, were it not for Bobby and Lyolya's strange behavior, I myself would have been pressing close to her and there would have been none of this scornful *froideur* or propriety. We at last came upon my beloved alley, black, forbidding, howling with the drone of invisible dry leaves, and it occurred to me that in such darkness, in such a sinister, secluded spot, there was bound to be some danger lurking (at the very least, a sudden attack) and that we, the two men, should have to forget our rivalry and join forces to defend Lyolya. As though bearing out these and similar thoughts of mine, somebody nearby shone a torch at us— emboldened like never before, I made ready to jump on him first, but the figure that drew into view was a tall gentleman in a smoking jacket, apparently making his peaceable way to the casino, and, in the light of his torch, with incontrovertible clarity, I saw Bobby embracing Lyolya with his free arm and caressing her—with immediate, instinctive cunning, I thought to lag behind a little (before the light vanished) and was just as incontrovertibly convinced that Lyolya, too, had her arm around Bobby.

I was struck by a desire to ask something caustic—"Well, how are you feeling now? Quite cozy?"—to prick them somehow, to show them that I saw and knew what was going on, but I feared the tension it would cause, the inopportunity of the words, and so, for the umpteenth time, I feebly held my tongue. The pain has not yet appeared, only the foresight of its duration, its immeasurable strength and implacability, some correspondence between it and what has happened today or may yet happen, and with each new blow I ask myself, with ever-growing amazement, how far will this pain go? how much more must I endure? while for now—before the pain comes—I feel recklessly and merrily intoxicated, as people do, listening to the swelling sounds of an orchestra as it drowns out a recognizable melody, or as they contemplate scandalous, destructive events, or even the very possibility of their own death—to spite someone, a stranger whom they blame for everything.

We turned around and, to warm ourselves, hurried along to the "grand opening." The event was a flop: the discerning bald Frenchman, who was there already with his bored companion, had been right, of course: there were indeed very few people in attendance. The casino resembled other such second-rate establishments—with a dining hall, a dance hall, two or three gaming rooms, and a terrace that had been made redundant by the inclement weather—everything had a phony, slapdash aura that masked something far more cobbled together, the tasteless décor somehow reminiscent of a Russian dacha. There appeared to be more organizers and employees (musicians, waiters, danseurs) than patrons, and while they imitated liveliness and good cheer as best they could, running hither and thither, dancing with one another and blowing industriously into their trumpets, the casino's proprietress, a youthful woman with auburn hair and a prodigious décolleté, met the guests on the terrace and reluctantly, scarcely concealing her chagrin, smiled at those others whom she had to let go, who had been frightened off by those vast, half-empty halls.

I invited Lyolya to dance a slow foxtrot with me—on occasion, we would pull it off rather well—but now she grimaced in annoyance:

"I'd rather we didn't go up first. Let's sit this one out."

But when Bobby asked her for the very next dance, she stood up and accompanied him without objection—Lyolya must have forgotten my invitation, overlooked it, for I am sure that she did not mean to offend me deliberately (whatever her feelings for Bobby may be), but it was that forgetfulness of hers that now enraged me, and childishly I promised myself never, but never to dance with her again.

All I could do was look at them and suddenly, accidentally discover how radiant they both were, how comfortable and well they looked together, both sitting and dancing.

There was something else that I observed, something that seemed even crueler to me: no sooner had they set off than their embrace became all the more brazen and unseemly, one cheek resting on another (I could even feel the vicarious touch of Lyolya's sweet, soft, velvety skin), and, after they came toward me, as though in cahoots with each other, as though conspiring together against me (I always resent that sense of lovers' complicity), they set off once more, but not before I spotted in Lyolya's eyes a long-familiar, sincere, somewhat misty gleam, which now seemed cruel and unforgiving. From this Lyolya, who was dangerous, so very hostile and alien to me, who had at last brought to bear what I had vaguely and blindly expected from the very outset—like an entranced animal that is lured by a plaintive cry into the trap that it has discovered—from this Lyolya's greedy summons, addressed to another, an overwhelming fear of helplessness came over me, the long-forgotten fear of childhood dreams—that I was sinking, that I had nobody to turn to, that nobody would come to my rescue. The pain, a real, physical pain—chills interspersed with nausea and faintness—has already reached me and found its way into everything (my head, my chest, my stomach), and there is yet another, indescribable pain—that caused by the fact that I shall never again sit with Lyolya, never get up and leave, never entreat or quarrel with her, by the same infidelity, the destructiveness of every step, every situation that I am faced with. Bobby and Lyolya carried on dancing, demanding applause, that the band play another number, and failing to notice how the remaining dancers dwindled. In the middle of one dance, Lyolya, still smiling, pushed Bobby away (I could already foresee something absolutely excruciating coming down the tracks) and quickly returned to her seat. They talked, as though I were invisible, gaily and tenderly—ever more like conspirators—and that fear of helplessness inside me grew ever more acute, as did the constant chills and pain. I could no longer think things through or reach decisions—my flickering, foreshortened thoughts were groping for something new and previously unnoticed in both my companions, something that had manifested itself so very suddenly but now could not be found: as ever, Bobby seemed to be wearing an inane grin and was only a little pinker than usual; Lyolya, on the other hand, was flushed, beaming with satisfaction and gratitude, and ravishing enough for two. Granted, she remained, as it were, entirely closed to me (as far as she was concerned, I was, quite simply, not there, and never once did she turn to me or notice that I, in my umbrage, would not dance with her, never did she appreciate my crestfallen silence), but this Lyolya, in thrall to dark, greedy impulses, isolated and withdrawn from me, I recalled perfectly—by other, already present signs, only I had failed to recognize their cruel, affronting combination. Other disparate, disfigured thoughts also flashed through my mind—why was Bobby here (or was all this torment not sooner the rule for me, my fate, and did Bobby in fact have nothing at all to do with this), and why did neither Lyolya nor any of the people around us seem to recognize that the three of us had come here as friends, that out of nowhere the two of them had conspired to torment me, the third wheel, that this was not decent behavior? I also tried to uncover the reason behind this unexpected favor: no matter how high I set myself, no matter how my tenacity, my inspired and necessary work moves me, inwardly I always register the successes of others, their victories over me, and I cannot settle for the excuse that I myself disdainfully refuse to fight, or that I am the victim of some misunderstanding or injustice (the perpetual mania of the defeated)—no, I persistently, instinctively seek out what it was that led my opponent to victory, what it was that I lacked, and so, as I looked at Bobby, stifled by the hopelessness and intractability of each passing moment, not knowing what to do with myself or where to hide—right now, at home, tomorrow—I somehow managed to stumble upon the semblance of an explanation, an unexpected question that suggested so much—why were Bobby and Lyolya both radiant while Zina and I were dull? and why, of the four of us, am I the only one who apparently does not know his place (by Zina's side)? But since a semblance of an explanation had been found—albeit in the law of outward consistency (not inner, mind, much as I should have liked to find it and much as it would have been truer)—I had inadvertently found my way out of a dead end (if only mentally, continuing all the while in my heart to mourn) and could now preserve some sorry dignity, forget about my fragility, and avoid courting pity: after all, the "law" cannot be changed. Then again, I did not even feel the urge to talk to Lyolya—because of the blind barrier that has sprung up between us and that is, moreover, clear to us both: in any friendship between two people, where one is somehow subordinate to the other (a son to a mother, a pupil to a teacher, a worker to his manager, one who is loving to another unloving), there comes a moment of danger when power begins to manifest itself, when friendship turns into control, a moment that is, for the subordinate, humiliating, painful, unforgivable—for me this rude change, this end to the usual warmth of friendship, this new imperious tone, the imposition of a new relationship is immensely difficult, instills long-running resentment, particularly where women are concerned, particularly where it is a matter of "loving" and "unloving," and such a cruel, arbitrary change, as Lyolya has had, always robs me of both courage and the hope of coming to some arrangement. To the bitter end, not once did I reproach Lyolya; the whole evening I spent in stubborn silence, evincing a certain irreproachability—back there in the alley, owing to a combination of awkwardness and wit-lessness, there in the ballroom, owing to fear, insult, maybe even a well-reasoned sense of despair—among the myriad reasons that had provoked this chance irreproachability were both my weakness and my strength.

Though I knew well (from past experience) that any attempt to shake off this lingering, miserable immobility was doomed to failure and would only lead (once a substitute had been found) back to a reality made even worse by the proven impossibility of escaping it, even so, to sit tight, to listen to Lyolya's gentle words (once addressed to me and so full of blissful meaning, but now, because of their repetition, because they have been handed on to Bobby, so ridiculous-sounding), to see her decidedly uncharacteristic attentions lavished every minute on a bewilderingly third-rate rival—no, this I could no longer endure, nor did I wish to do so, and so I waited for a convenient pretext to get up and leave—one that was credible, not cutting or provocative. I had long already been eying up our Russian neighbor (with that imperceptible and, nevertheless, prying concentration with which people who appear to be absorbed in their own woes see and commit to memory every little outside trifle accompanying them), so pale and mirthless, intending all the while to dance with her; I even harbored the dubious hope of riling Lyolya with this, but then there was the danger of refusal, after which would come my exposure and indisputable, definitive despair. Then again, matters could not get any worse, and, besides, the Russian lady was smiling at me encouragingly, so I made up my mind there and then—with a sense of mortal risk (perhaps posturing a little into the bargain)—to go up to her. As I got to my feet, blushing on account of my belated appeal, I said far too brazenly and in an unaccountably loud voice:

"Lyolya, you won't mind if I invite someone else to dance, will you? Our neighbor, for instance?"

"By all means."

Without a moment's hesitation, the Russian lady stretched out her hand amicably, affectionately even, as though to a respectable, eccentric, and unduly shy admirer, while the Frenchman smiled at me, pleased to see her amused and clearly having discussed the three of us with her already. In the middle of the dance, my partner suddenly and with a naïve show of sympathy asked:

"Why were you sitting there so forlorn, while your friends were having a jolly time?"

She danced marvelously, leading imperceptibly and in perfect step with me (I myself am an uneven dancer, forever at the mercy of my partner), responding to every caprice and quickening of the music. She seemed to lack any bones (she was at once putty in my hands, and yet possessed of an almost balletic poise); I glided after her, admiring her unceasingly suggestive flexibility, and was ready to transfer my admiration onto anything else that she might have to offer, even to compare her limp conversation with Lyolya's, especially with today's, hostile as it was, but it was in her conversation that I divined something long-familiar and, next to Lyolya, irredeemably gray—the young ladies' institute, the provinces, the superficial sheen of Paris. Very likely it would have been amusing to ask her about the conversation that I had overheard in the café by the lake, about my incensed speculations—if only Lyolya had listened to me then with her usual attention—but now I feared losing the last visible remnants of my dignity and decided not to let myself be drawn, lest it remind me of Lyolya's humiliating aloofness. When I, after thanking the Russian lady and her patron much too effusively, returned to Lyolya in trepidation (vaguely hoping that everything would suddenly change), I found her sitting there as before, distant, flushed, misty-eyed, and seeming to notice neither my presence, nor the deliberate, immoderate plaudits from my new acquaintance.

I decided to take a wander through the bright, empty halls and was stopped by the auburn hostess in her décolleté at the only card table where there were people playing—she persuaded me to join them, in doing which she revealed herself to be no fool, but much too artless and frankly avaricious: for some reason, she put me in mind of the ginger dancer at the restaurant I had patronized together with Lyolya and on the eve of her arrival, and, as I compared both these luridly seductive women to Lyolya, I satisfied myself once again of her resplendent irreplaceability, one that was, as far as I was concerned, now lost, squandered, for I felt myself consumed entirely, emptied even, when I unwittingly compared our first evening together, and how the dancer had paled before Lyolya, and how I had delighted in this, believing that I had won Lyolya, or at least that she was destined for me—if only as a friend—with this evening, this hopeless, unforgettable turning point. While I conversed with the hostess, I could see Lyolya and Bobby dancing again in the distance, and I felt myself drawn toward the ballroom—but not into the room itself, and not to my seat—so that I should be able to observe them safely and unnoticed, not missing a single movement, a telling smile, hitting upon some—doubtless bitter—truth, only then to tell myself: I am no longer with Lyolya, though she may not know it, and though she may well be indifferent to the fact—this is how I shall prove myself shrewder and more dignified, and only thereby shall I have any peace. There were, in fact, more than sufficient grounds for the break (if one can call it such, this private, unilateral decision for which Lyolya cares nothing and to which it would be ridiculous of her to admit), yet I retain the craven hope that I am mistaken, that I have simply done something to upset Lyolya, that she is being capricious, and that tomorrow everything will be as it was before; if, however, I were to stop believing in such arrant nonsense, I should still seek—conscious of my own impotence—to pin the blame on something indisputable and unforgivable, lest I live to regret the mistake, while to find the strength to make the break now, in a blaze of indignant anguish, would mean not seeing each other, or leaving Paris altogether. As I stood in a room leading off from the ballroom, in the midst of a certain commotion at the snack bar, I saw Lyolya and Bobby now right before me, now reflected in various mirrors, while I myself, with ostensible indifference, drank Bénédictine and Curaçao—sometimes they would draw close, almost bearing down on me, silently clinging to each other with weary affection, and yet thus far I had seen nothing that might console me, nor indeed anything that was indisputably amiss.

We returned home along the autumn streets, which recalled the desolation of our Russian countryside; Lyolya and Bobby walked arm in arm, while I, resentful, pressed on ahead, guiding them with as few words as were necessary. Other than my strangled directions, not a word was spoken, and it seemed to me that Lyolya was maintaining an especially stubborn silence—doubtless, she had been reticent to strike up conversations with me even in former times, but now it was so wanting, so hurtfully unlike the contrition, the passionate remorse that had given me vague reassurance all evening, that it was as if I failed to notice, to catch her indifferent words. Like others who are weak or in some way enfeebled, my miserable attention was concentrated not on the general (that Lyolya prefers Bobby over me), but on the latest, minor (albeit telling) trifle—why now was Lyolya, as she walked beside me, knowing full well how much it would hurt me, clinging fast to Bobby's arm and not to mine, or—in camaraderie—to both his and mine at once? There was clearly no fault in my reasoning, although for me it was frankly humiliating: everything was over, Lyolya had given me the slip, cheated me, unwittingly betrayed me; I am prepared to tolerate and accept any inevitable wrongdoing, but why was she causing such excessive, easily avoidable torment? It was Bobby who unexpectedly broke these morbid, self-indulgent thoughts of mine with an ill-judged question, one that seemed bizarre in the midst of our solemn silence:

"Oh, I forgot to tell you. My old man has received a rather interesting proposition. It's just the thing for Derval. We just have to run a few checks on their *bilan* first."

I do not know whether Bobby had divined my growing hostility or had really recollected some possible business venture; in either case, it struck me that he, the victor, was trying to engage me in conversation out of a sense of pity, and this put my back up—my anger had until then been directed mostly at Lyolya (this is what she had done to me)—and at the same time I realized, gloatingly, with a certain malicious joy, that Bobby had made a fool of himself, that he could not but make a fool of himself, that not only were his clueless Gallicisms ridiculous and absurd, but so too was this preposterous act of his, that Lyolya must have understood all this perfectly, that such a nonentity could never be the object of love or jealousy, and so I composed myself and only shuddered as we approached our sleepy *pension*—after all, the long night (which has somehow escaped my memory) spread out before us, and so with it countless fears and their cruel familiarity, forgotten and revived many times over, like bouts of a slow, sometimes subsiding, yet all the same incurable and hateful illness. Unbearable memories of Lyolya flashed instantly before my eyes, each one alike the next—my old jealousy toward her husband (which now seemed perfectly puerile), her at times sinister inscrutability, which I felt keenly, and which led her away from me, her dazzling feminine splendor—and all my fear, all my uncertain jealousy, my helplessness (the invariably sad consequences of our love and unlovability) suddenly materialized in Bobby, grinning, clumsy, all-powerful, in those silly *pension* rooms, in that improbable night that I was forced to suffer (after which I would be fine, I would change, forget, run away), that night that, like a mousetrap, suddenly ensnared me, overwhelmed me, cruelly cut me off from outside help, so that I could not escape the inevitable mockery and torment.

Only after some quite persistent ringing of the bell did we gain entry and make our way quietly upstairs—all three of us—to Lyolya's room. Lyolya lay down on the bed, while Bobby sat at her feet and I—with a certain defiance—collapsed in the only armchair, anxiously waiting to see whether Bobby would so much as graze the tip of Lyolya's toe. Watching them resentfully, vigilantly, and with hostility, I concocted (as any person would in a hopeless situation) the most unlikely means of escaping this desperation and guaranteeing for myself some quiet hours before morning, and my mind came to rest on one means in particular, an especially clumsy and desperate rouse that was prompted by my old dealings with Lyolya, by our former intimacy, which I have hardly mentioned until now. My veil of silence has been by no means accidental: I have always imagined that my notebooks may someday fall into the hands of another (it has always horrified me to think that Zina or some curious acquaintance waiting for me might pick them up, or that, in a fog after hours of grueling labor, I might carelessly forget them in some café); I have never given them to another to read, nor do I even have anybody to whom I might show them, but I wanted to keep alive the hope, the prospect that I may yet find an understanding reader, some "appraiser" selected by me—then I should have the time to tear out the only dangerous page (stashing it away, of course, for myself) and to cross out a few unnecessary words. Considerations of gentlemanliness notwithstanding, and likewise my reluctance to lay bare my own private affairs, I was simply afraid to put into cumbersome, revealing words the vast difference between what people understand by a harmonious, romantic intimacy and what we had together; but more importantly, such candor was hampered by my constant reckoning with Lyolya, by a certain physical and mental clamming up, which happened even when she was not physically present in the room—this unrewardable irreproachability of mine in her absence surprised and touched me: after all, never once did I speak of Lyolya or commit to paper (perhaps the thought never even occurred to me, so wholly was I consumed by her) those unavoidably treacherous opinions about a person who is absent—however true or insignificant they may be—which might have caused Lyolya offense and driven her away from me (I need not count the vindictive thoughts, the whole painful arena of "Lyolya and me"—each imaginary conversation that I had with her turned out to be either a complaint or an appeal to love me). But now Lyolya has been the first to break our comradely sense of loyalty, our bond of reciprocal clemency, the kindness so characteristic of our relationship, and now I am no longer minded to make allowances for her, to maintain my irreproachability, to repress anything in myself that she finds objectionable; no, I am quite prepared—naturally, without crude and indifferent witnesses—to declare right here, in this very notebook, at a most significant time for me, as sincerely and mercilessly as possible: yes, Lyolya and I were once close, and even if she did pity me, overcoming her indifference, yet she could never deny this intimacy, nor ever take it from my memory, which in its audacity has preserved and can so easily retrieve the incomparable enchantment of our many evenings spent together—how Lyolya, without embarrassment (like a wife before her husband), would throw off her dress, unfasten her stockings, and slowly reappear in front of me, a new woman, thrillingly tangible and yet unfathomable, a tiny, tender angel, suddenly warm and now irresistibly feminine and seductive. It feels odd to write down everything about Lyolya that previously seemed forbidden, sacrilegious, simply impossible, but I am accustoming myself to this, and the act itself has at last prompted me—in Lyolya's room, when the three of us were together, amid my mutinous despair—to try disregarding her in the open and, no matter her own wishes, to foist on her our own now-salutary past—such was the pathetic, absurd means, dreamed up in a single moment, by which I hoped to avoid a long, lonely night of jealousy and incessant eavesdropping, a jealousy that was, alas, justified: I decided—even though Lyolya and I, after Sergei N.'s first letter from abroad, had never spent the night together (I can think of no better way to put it), and had since then (granted, without having agreed to it in so many words) always gone our own separate ways in the evening—I decided to feign ignorance and, as a naïve warning to Lyolya, to ensconce myself, or rather not to leave her side.

All of a sudden, Bobby, without having said a word to us and only making a comic gesture of resignation (he had won, was free to do as he pleased, and hence was playing the magnanimous victor), disappeared behind the door, giving me a chance to warn Lyolya of my decision, but I was already vaguely aware of the pointlessness of such an attempt and began to yield to the understandable desire to put it off, to the suicidal spirit of abandon and indolence. We both of us remained silent; with an incorrigible submissiveness, I waited for Bobby's hurried steps, and soon enough I thought I distinctly heard them, but it turned out to have been a mistake, and here the momentary ordeal of bitterness and fear for what had been lost imbued me with the courage to address a few hasty words to Lyolya:

"It's high time we all went to bed. We'll retire shortly, and I'll come straight back. If you'll permit me, that is."

She stared at me, first with a look of dissatisfied surprise (as though she had suddenly been woken up, and for no good reason), and then, indicating the door significantly, with a look of affront and reproach, one that said to me, no, it's unseemly for two to conspire to deceive a third. I could have reminded her of her own quite recent and not at all dissimilar culpability in that regard, but I was seemingly dumbstruck with fear, with the mortal need to reconcile, and after this first exchange—albeit strange and mute—I no longer accused Lyolya of anything and instead felt the need to justify myself to her, contriving something absurd and limply believing in my own invention:

"Maybe you're right. I only wanted to have a little chat with you."

Our rooms were on the same corridor but separated from one another; Bobby's room, more to the point, was situated between mine and Lyolya's, so it was simply impossible for me to hear anything going on in her room. True, I did listen nevertheless with an intense, unrelenting, likely unerring keenness, like a burglar or a soldier on reconnaissance, risking life and limb, but there is an obvious limit to what a person can do, and, no matter how I persevered, I was unable to determine anything conclusively. At times it seemed to me as if I were mastering myself and reading my book attentively, whereas in actual fact—being absent—I was skimming the words and leafing through its pages, and, when at last I forced myself to pay attention, I found that I despised (and today I despise it yet) the elevated, prophetically dry, lifeless tone of this much-vaunted work—I was reading *Les Nourritures terrestres*, an undertaking that I shall never repeat, even though the reason for its incomprehensibility and my loathing, of course, lay in me, and even though in other circumstances I find myself much affected by André Gide and capable of learning something from him. Now and then I would hear (as is inevitable in such moments) some alarming, odious noises, and then, unable to endure the pain of suspicion, after so many sensible attempts to escape it (in some seemingly deliberate sequence, as though trying to satisfy myself that the sensible attempts had not been enough), I sought help in certain desperate fictions that briefly consoled me from this agony: I imagined myself softly stealing through the garden to Lyolya's half-open window, seeing "everything" clearly, and then, having ensured, having prepared the way for Lyolya's absolute humiliation, spitefully and imperiously, no longer stealing, but bursting into her room from the corridor, tearing off the duvet, and Lyolya, caught in the act, red-handed, suddenly straightening up and looking me in the eye with proud, cruel, almost shameless defiance. Next, my imagination divided in two—either, having learned the bitter truth, I would leave Lyolya once and for all, only for her to realize that she would have to make do with Bobby alone, or else she would drive Bobby out forthwith, holding me back, and we should passionately and touchingly make our peace (there was, of course, a third option—hardly considered, lazy, quickly dismissed: my vindictive suicide)—in each of these cases, Lyolya would be proved wrong and put to shame, while I, every time (and each in a different way) would triumph. Gradually, I became so used to all these imaginary possibilities (and in particular to their identical beginning—in the garden, by Lyolya's window) that I decided not to undress, fearing to miss such a patently far-fetched hope, nor to credit the famous saying about the early bird, the pale sky, or the impending abandonment of hope. I tried to go to sleep only after the first light, but soon—lacking the courage to lie there in the light and remain deathly still—I got up and went out to wander the streets, which were unrecognizably clean and tidy, trying to think calmly and rationally how I should now extricate myself from my present desperation, if only to put an end to the torments, blows, and insults of this humiliating and undeserved night. Having ventured off a long way, I suddenly remembered, reckoned that Lyolya would probably be awake already, and so I rushed back without thinking, with a single aim in mind, one that betokened new agonizing nights and new humiliations—to see Lyolya as soon as possible.

When, after knocking, I entered her room, I found Bobby and Lyolya sitting at either end of an already made-up bed, both of them unbearably radiant and contented—in a kind of harmonious, brazen, exceedingly friendly pose (each of them attending to their morning manicure)—and once again I had occasion to see for myself how relaxed and happy they were together, although I still managed to calm myself a little, for I had hungered for Lyolya, and now, having got my hands on her (failing to recall at once her iniquity—grateful, blind, reckless as I was), I slowly imbibed her presence.

I HAVE FOUND it more difficult than ever to force myself to write—it seemed impossible to tear myself away from my passionate, feverish preoccupation with Lyolya and to drag my innumerable, incoherent observations through the blur of those two days at Blainville: what captivates us, even fleetingly, rends us unavoidably from everything else, and until recently I had thought it a great feat to be able to commit my sudden rush of emotion, the excitement from Lyolya's proximity in a telephone booth, to pages in a notebook— now all that seems impossibly charmed and so very easy. In despair, in jealousy, in such impatience as I feel now, suspicious every minute, when shaving or taking dinner are harrowing experiences and, as it were, lead me away from what is essential—namely, not to leave Bobby and Lyolya alone together, to be ever on the alert when I am with them, to catch every scarcely perceptible change that takes place—in such unbridled fever, in which to find the strength if only to maintain my dignity and not to reveal my humiliating afflic- tion, and in which to find such immeasurable strength to sit there for a long while, to set in order the mad onslaught of thoughts and events, simply to lead my pen across the paper.

After we arrived back from Blainville—yesterday—Lyolya said that she was tired and wanted to go to bed early, while Bobby and I, hostile and taciturn, parted ways on her door- step; another sleepless night lay in store for me—I went home and, without anything particular in mind, electing not to frighten myself unnecessarily with the impending yet inevitable ennui and anxiety, I threw down my notebook on the table, spread it open, and began writing immediately. More and more, I became absorbed in the act of writing (more, in fact, than ever before); I made recollections, judgments, comparisons; I paced back and forth endlessly along the narrow little rug—lest my steps make a noise—and gradually I managed to calm myself (with a touch of childishness, as though I had had a good cry and a good snivel, before finally settling down). I was very likely helped by the fact that there was no chance of my seeing Lyolya until the following morning, and so it was no use agonizing or snooping around—in any event, after yesterday's scribblings I have in reserve enough composure and concentration, enough self-renewing inner curiosity, for today's. True, by morning, as soon as I stopped writing, the unnaturalness and desperation of this miserable distraction was immediately revealed to me: yet again I had not slept, and yet again I had tormented myself—setting down what I had retained and found in my memory, carrying out the task I had set myself—stubbornly, foolishly, and to no avail. On the other hand, I do now have a vague renewed sense of pride—that I am cracking the whip unsparingly, that I have translated, that I can translate one state of mind into another and, more to the point, even at a time when I am in the grip of unrelenting, indomitable pain, when I have succumbed to it and can no longer offer up any resistance, and when the first thrust of effort entails all the violence and vigor of a surgeon—and together with this pride in what I have achieved comes the age-old question, one that is natural, eternal, and without answer, one of fairness and reward: will it really ever vanish from the world?—not the pain of loving, which I know well and continues yet, but this very endeavor—imposed who knows by whom, tormenting me and draining me of all strength—to acknowledge that pain, and to put it into words.

My second and final day at Blainville was even more miserable and loathsome than the first, and so ridiculously unlike what I had envisaged and what I had promised Lyolya. Late in the afternoon, Bobby, as he had done on the previous day, again went to make a telephone call. He returned terribly upset:

"Everything's working out splendidly for you. My old man asked me to tell you that Derval says the paperwork is almost ready." (This should have been my greatest success, but even this news could not banish the pain and loathing and only raised the kind of inner smirk that it would have done in anybody in such circumstances—what else is money and wanton success good for?) "But things aren't so grand *chez nous*. Zina is very ill and they're leaving tomorrow morning at ten. This could spell disaster for our plans—I'm afraid the old boy will bungle the whole thing."

"Perhaps you'd better go with Zina. That way, your father can see to the business affairs and take your place later."

This suggestion of mine seemed—to me, at least—quite apropos and, on the face of it at least, sensitive to Bobby's distress and panic, although of course it derived not from any sympathy, but from a certain sense of malicious joy, from the fleeing hope that I might forget all about him, even if only for a while, along with his outrageous behavior those past few days—making me play the detective, drawing humiliating, importunate, jealous comparisons, comparisons that are uncharitable, always hurtful, and quite unnecessary. Lyolya apparently managed to fathom the nefarious intent behind my ostensibly friendly interference and, enraged by this, with a tremor in her voice, objected:

"You aren't going anywhere, Bob. These illnesses are no laughing matter, so let your father take care of things like the grown man that he is, and, God willing, the business affairs will take care of themselves."

I was mortified that Lyolya had caught me out, likewise that her outburst had been so indignant, so vitriolic toward me, and that it had betrayed such deep, tender affection for Bobby: her devotion to him seemed remarkably unfair, as did her sweet, motherly care—no matter what befell him, Bobby forever remained exactly the same, a nonentity without a single distinguishing feature, a mediocrity without even good or wicked intent, a nobody who spoke in foreign, approximate words, apparently unable to deceive anybody. I had at the ready any number of objections that Lyolya would have found insulting, objections that were, at any rate, substantial enough: that it was only because of our ridiculous rivalry that I had become unchivalrous in my dealings with Bobby; that Lyolya herself had fashioned that artificial rivalry in the first place; that she, with her vulgar and provocative behavior, had awakened my sense of *amour-propre*, which had been lacking in the bygone days of our more equal partnership, and which could no longer be placated and stood only to sour me against any other prospective suiter of hers; that one simply cannot—sans reason or explanation—treat people with such thoughtlessness. Of course, I kept a feeble silence, but I was so incensed, so filled with rage—so much in fact that for a time I was delivered from my mistrustful jealousy, from the maniacal need to observe them every minute that they were with me, and to imagine what they got up to in my absence, and in a daze, barely holding back the tears, I went out into the garden, where I spent a long time pacing around, thinking up ever newer and more scathing lines of argument with which to destroy Lyolya. Perhaps it was not only her perspicacity, nor even her condemnation of my unraveled advice, that hurt me and forced me to make excuses and go on the attack, but also something that all this concealed, something that had reared its head previously and was, very likely, anathema to Lyolya: with inexplicable regularity I find myself cast together with victors and persecutors, siding with them in fortune, might, and arrogance; I myself am at times possessed of brute strength and am able to regard the defeated and wretched with a detached, almost curious sense of indifference, and without the least pity or warmth. I so desperately wanted to reply that the human struggle really does not interest me all that much, that I am just as incurious about my victorious allies as I am about my own worldly success, and that I am not ashamed of my at times brutal strength, which inevitably passes, only to be replaced, as it has been now, by a sense of frailty—in this case, one that derives from Lyolya and is, perforce, all-consuming. I returned to the balcony where I had left Lyolya and Bobby and, of course, said nothing of what I had prepared, so certain was I of my defeat, and so I decided, since I could expect no help, no protection, no vindication from Lyolya, that it was for me to outwit and stave off the desperation of that evening, that night, our last in Blainville (because of Zina's impending departure), a night that seemed singularly dangerous.

After lunch, feeling as though I were committing some irreparable deed and, with a certain spiteful exhilaration, trying to act as naturally and nonchalantly as possible, I announced, as though in passing:

"I'm sorry, truly, but I must leave at once, and I may be gone quite some time."

Lyolya looked up at me strangely, as though on the cusp of realizing what I was up to and meaning to stop me. I am convinced that I was not mistaken in this, but after so many blows and disappointments I could not compose myself without conducting a new experiment—and a last, lingering smile from Lyolya would have altered my mood for the entire evening. When, as I was leaving the garden, I looked back at the balcony, Lyolya was not looking in my direction (as I had expected) and was laughing gaily with Bobby, immediately dispelling my hopes for even the most dubious kind of loyalty. Once again, I set out to wander down that long-familiar path, somewhat buoyed by the fact that the bitter monotony of those days in Blainville had been broken (a monotony that pretended to eternity, just like any ghastly present) and that I was at last alone with myself, having of my own accord torn myself away from Lyolya, able to take a proper look at what had gone on, and, with a slow clarity—unmolested by the nagging ache of jealousy—to ponder calmly and rationally how I might deliver myself from this bondage, how I might become—however miserably, however grudgingly—free. The walk, the solitude, and the thinking, however, soon seemed ridiculous and unbearable, and I felt drawn once again to people, to the casino, where even the previous night I had distinguished something vaguely animating and agreeable, and where Lyolya and Bobby, by my reckoning (because of Zina's departure, and so as to be alone together), would not show their faces—and even if they did, I would show Lyolya just how easy it was to get by without her (much later, weary from all that feigned exuberance, I was obsessed by the thought of Lyolya's arrival, of a reprise of that miracle at the bistro, when in the space of a minute her hopelessly late appearance placated the long hours of my despair).

The casino stood empty, as before, and guests were few and far between—the Franco-Russian couple, the gentleman in the smoking jacket, who on the previous evening had so frightened us in the alley, and another group who were placing small bets on a game of boules. I invited the hostess to sit with me for a while and soon, to her great surprise and proprietorial delight, began to intoxicate myself with an array of various liqueurs in turn, trying to avoid that ambiguous, transitional state: I envisaged that inspired sense of elation that sometimes comes with inebriation at the hand of despair but is often just missed because of the sluggishness or inertia of the transition. Intoxication came quickly, however—it is forever associated for me with the psychological state that precedes it, almost accentuating it, pinpointing it, or, if I cannot put my finger on it, underscoring it, but this connection with my recent past, the emphasis on it, can be especially harsh, if that past is hopeless, if I am ill, mentally crippled, so completely constrained that I cannot breathe, while drunkenness liberates my sorry past, casting off the veil of some barren, lengthy immobility, revealing all the creative tension and strength that despair entails and that will someday take their toll. And so now, as usual, I succumbed to the ostensibly quickening movement around me and was imbued with a feeling of benevolence for all these people, but this was not some chance drunken folly, one born of love and nonsense— the sort that I often experience and can identify at the drop of a hat—no, this was, to be specific, a liberation, an eruption of hidden, buried, tender feelings, feelings that had been misplaced, that had reached nobody and had been accepted by none: that same feeling of despair persisted, unbroken and unremittingly palpable, yet it withdrew, alleviated somewhat, as though obscured by the nice people around me and by my fraternal, sympathetic feelings of friendship toward them. Such contentment in the midst of despair (or equally a sad glance in the fullness of happy love) is the redemptive contradiction that leads us away from the animal, the thoughtless, the voiceless thrall to subsequent, sometimes lofty, possibilities: poignant conclusions and their poetic revelation, the necessary fortitude in life's struggle (which, next to this, seems demonstrably petty), and even a certain indifference to death; mentally (and not monetarily) we are often generous; the richer we are, the more generous we become, and then—without greed, without regret—we find ourselves ready to give up what is ours, and even our very selves. Granted, this contentment of mine seems somewhat artificial, inebriated, accidental, but I know from long experience that it is none other than this inebriation that crowns our hopelessness, our love, everything within us that is fruitful and awaiting expression; it lingers on in our soul's memory, and I know that the words and thoughts to which it gives rise are often disjointed and erratic, but at heart they are refreshingly true. There, in the casino, I came unhesitatingly—with courage and inspiration—to the realization that my despair had only just begun and would be yet greater than in those first days—the most unendurable blow for a lover is that which is yet to come, although one must live in the constant expectation of it—but, all the same, there will be bouts of contentment similar to this, even if they are forcibly produced, and they will grow, envelop, and gradually displace my despair, and from them I shall extract the strength to share in the movement of life itself, with old age, disgraceful failures, and petty, foolish aims, to experience it with tenfold enthusiasm and, as it were, to enjoy it from without. I also had a premonition that after the despair, after having made my peace with it, a sense of friendship would remain, one that did not require evidential proofs, splendid words, vociferous addresses, but contented itself with gestures, tenderness, a tenor, an air of courtesy and brotherhood. I must have begun to broadcast these thoughts unconsciously even then, amid the inebriation (and, indeed, not only because of the inebriation)—I myself was surprised to discover this in the appreciative and trusting warmth of the responses, when I gathered almost everybody around my table—the hostess, the Russian lady, the Frenchman with the rosette (I revealed to him that I had overheard his excusably ignorant conversation about Russia) and the gentleman in the smoking jacket, who enquired sympathetically about Lyolya and seemed healthy, composed, well-protected against an affliction such as mine, and, given this protection, I was touched by his sympathy, by his offer of support in my own affliction. We drank copiously, but I remained as alert as ever, paying careful, devoted

attention to my newfound companions and forever returning to the same point—to the miracle of this prospective
epiphany after Lyolya's impending departure, strange and
unendurable though it seemed. To content myself with my
original explanation suddenly appeared (as is often the
case) ridiculously inadequate and naïve: thoughts that had
been inadvertently set in motion rushed uncontrollably,
alarming and seducing me with an all-permitting, intimate,
half-grasped elegance—to those former thoughts (about the
necessary renunciation of the animalistic fullness of sensa-
tions, about the humanizing and creative power of rejection)
something willful had now been added, something that
drew comparisons and made calculations. I approached it
as though from afar, and my reasoning ran roughly thus: if
everything flops and comes crashing down on you, you will
eventually tire of indignation and only turn your cheek,
although an undeniable feeling of guilt will remain—that you
lack the power to deter, the "reins," a sense of proportion—
yet this feeling, this guilt, will rear its head even when your
luck is in (at the card table, with women, in your career),
when, unable to stave off fate, you have so confidently taken
everything for granted, and then you will find yourself
obliged, compelled even, to let go a part of that luck, but it is
not misfortune in its entirety that crashes down, nor are you
entombed by it; so must you not allow luck to unravel you,
nor yourself to lash out blindly and predatorily, but rather
you must learn to brace yourself, to step aside, as it were, and

there shall you find yourself in a realm of unceasing mental effort, one that rebels against totality, wholeness, sweet, blissful self-dissolution—therein lies, in a modest way, from the bottom up, without any rash faith, without divine grace, the only possible ascension that is achievable by man, an ascension that is unspeakably arduous, one that failure threatens by the minute, one in which the infinitely powerful, inimitable upward flight of an individual human soul has more meaning and value than the cumbersome and weighty movement of "society" (which is slow and will never catch up with it), than any superficially heroic act—one that is wingless, dumb, and able to be accomplished by a savage and a child alike.

Even now I bear a trace of that drunken evening, of its dulcet charm (the trace disappeared, inexplicably, only after Zina had been seen off, when some understanding, sympathetic kindness was especially called for); some feeling of reconciliation remains, although absurd and unfortunate circumstances—the fact that I am too often busy, that Lyolya is not always available, that she and Bobby take pains to meet without me—lead me to such helplessness, chase me into such a vice-like trap from which I seemingly cannot escape, yet it just so happens that helplessness like this also bolsters my sense of reconciliation: I cannot interfere with anything and, therefore, I have no cause to fight, and it was not without reason that I rushed from Blainville back to my, oh, so dubious sense of Parisian security, apparently anticipating that

I should be able to write there—fear, you see, makes writing impossible, as it did before Lyolya left for Berlin—for I find writing to be not only a useful and distracting enterprise, but also a means, perhaps the only means, of speaking freely about what matters most to me, whereas with Lyolya, for whom all this "what matters" is carefully and pointlessly kept, there is obligation, excessive, frightened consideration, and enslavement.

October 2

ONCE AGAIN, I appear to be caught in a rut—one that seems fixed and unalterable—but I need only imagine myself as I was recently and the view I should then have taken of myself as I am now, and it becomes simply incomprehensible to me how I could have permitted such a humiliating change to take place. I have been stricken by an affliction to which I have grown accustomed, as one accustoms oneself to the dark or ennui, an affliction that from day to day does not prevent me from doing (hastily and haphazardly) anything that a healthy person might—being fastidious, kind, careful with money—but all this hardly touches me, and I find it only easier to pass over any hindrance or blunder, since they do not affect anything that matters. What does matter, on the other hand, what began back then in Blainville, became intractable, and has perhaps since then become—owing to habit, time, despair—a little less keen, is that I am sick with jealousy: that, and Lyolya's disfavor. I spend entire days at her hotel, and I know no calm unless I am there—it forever seems to me that something irreparable will happen without me there, that I suicidally abet this "something irreparable" with every hour of my absence. I have long detested the hotel lobby where I am made to wait eternally for Lyolya (*"madame descend tout de suite"*), but all the same, it does have a certain calming quality in comparison to the street or my room, which are located somewhere in another world, one quite unconnected to Lyolya. We are rarely alone—Lyolya avoids this, insofar as she is able, and often, on various pretexts, disposes of me, whereas I am so accustomed, so habituated to this humiliation, I so fear giving Lyolya cause for quarrel or not to receive me, that I hardly appear to notice it. It is Bobby who usually impinges on our would-be solitude, and the worst of it is that I, taking advantage of Lyolya's patience (and, perhaps, her well-bred sense of tact), prevent them in turn from secluding themselves, caring nothing that my sorry station is only too apparent to them (sparing no thought whatsoever for my bond of friendship or for that same much-needed sense of tact), and I only rejoice when I leave together with Bobby, able to rest assured that at least they are not together and no treachery is being committed. If, on the other hand, Lyolya and I ever find ourselves alone together, on that rarest of occasions, we are silent, or else pick over such trivial things that mean nothing to us, smiling limply at each other now and then, and this is so staggeringly unlike that first mutual curiosity, those former conversations of ours, full of hasty, insatiable questions, answers that feverishly awaited approval, the indescribable charm of that shared approval and respect. There was a time when Lyolya was proud of our intelligent and equal-footed friendship and believed it to be crucial for us both; perhaps she still holds it to be so even now and feels as though she needs to make excuses to herself—and partly to me—for the hurtful change that has taken place. She occasionally makes insinuations:

"No friendship can withstand the passage of time. Sooner or later, people will finish saying whatever it is that they have to say, and then you'll know everything a priori—there won't be a single thing left to surprise you. Maybe it's different for people who just don't pay attention or aren't perceptive enough, but really that isn't friendship."

Lyolya is wrong, of course: it is that first flush of curiosity, that exchange of superficial appraisals that is not really friendship, and those who settle for it are not in fact inclined to friendship, or else are spiritually impoverished, but there are certain people, very few—and only in rare, selected cases, at that—who have the almost boundless ability to venture further, toward mutual inspiration, quick and easy tacit understanding, the subconscious, unerring ability to help, guide even, and such a relationship between two people is never exhausted, nor can it be broken off (at least, not on purpose, not by design or whim), although there can also be something sobering in the awareness of being responsible for somebody, especially somebody quick-witted and hence mistrustful, and even though there will inevitably come an of course temporary period of natural dissatisfaction, one that arises from the fatigue of unrelenting strain. Nothing will come of my relationship with Lyolya, however; not because we are spiritually impoverished or not disposed toward friendship (I am dispensing with all modesty here), but because there is no friendship between us, and I am always ready for Lyolya's criticisms and ridicule, I am always anxious, watching my every word, I commit to memory the great multitude of my likely successful remarks that in former times Lyolya would have gratifyingly endorsed, but which I now swallow, lest she find, lest she suspect some inference that irritates her—and I only regret the relative freedom with which I would, even recently, write to her. Our encounters are spoiled also by the very presence of a third person, by the fact that any friendship, union, conversation is diluted by the intrusion of new participants: to any friend or vis-à-vis we show a particular side of ours, one that they will find interesting and that will touch them, whereas a friendship or a conversation with several people is the combined force of all such unilateral aspirations of ours, the result of all our individual parts, each of which is, moreover, immeasurably less than the whole and must be made to conform at once to a great many dissimilar people, thereby diminishing and anonymizing us. Some find it easy to attune themselves to this, for which they need an inner flexibility and speed, the kind that an orator has, for instance, or somebody widely regarded as a wit or "the life and soul of the party." I have the opposite, intolerable disadvantage of appreciating, with a certain exaggerated sense of shame, the whole artificiality of such situations, the folly of seeking them out, the futility of all that effort, and I prefer conversations—where any third party is present—that are indifferent and blasé, leaving anything of real substance to tête-à-têtes. What is simply beyond me is the knack for dealing with Bobby and Lyolya when they are together (dealing with each of them alone is difficult enough), and, after however many blunders, I can now see almost graphically how my pitiful attempts to find the right tone for one and the other (friendly and light-hearted for Bobby, and ironically afflicted for Lyolya) cross each other but never converge, and how I attempt to ingratiate myself, as it were, with each of them by turns, trying to land on a much-sought-after middle tone. I am also disturbed by the incessant radiance that continues to emanate from them, a radiance that is powerful beyond measure and much too coordinated if they are nearby. I never cease to be aware how clever, how cheerful, how charming Lyolya is—enough for two—or how she fails to notice Bobby's tedious clumsiness. At her every elegant posture (she apparently knows how to strike them like nobody else), at her every vivacious, instinctively deadly look, at Bobby's every gaffe, I am quite ready to boil over with rage because of this whole mismatch and injustice, as if I were witnessing an old man marrying a young girl. Sometimes I feel a growing sense of indignation, not only on my own account, but also on Sergei N.'s, who did so much for Lyolya and who has been so cheaply, so summarily replaced by Bobby, and then I begin to feel twice the anger, twice the anguish, twice the abhorrence. Sergei N.'s victory, his triumph, would have been a deliverance for me (doubtless there is a similar joy—that in the lesser evil—to be had when the husband of the woman we love, a man who is ready to make any sacrifice and to endure anything for her sake, trounces and sends packing some smooth-talking cad who has been telling of his conquests with a grin). Besides, Sergei N.'s victory is the victory of my chaste beginning with Lyolya over Bobby's hateful one—I have finally understood the source of his enduring charms. But this victory is yet to come, and any prospective rapprochement between me and Sergei N. would be comic and humiliating, the rapprochement of philosophizing losers who have been punished by somebody who can, who by his very nature knows how to inspire love—truly and without sophistication. I have also understood at last that both Sergei N. and I were Lyolya's attempts to raise her prospects, while Bobby and her husband before him speak to her base, passionate reality, that no "union" (as I previously imagined) will ever now take place, and that Lyolya will have to content herself with the singularly coarse and tedious Bobby, who could never unite anything and is just the ticket for her.

But now, I, too, find myself in a base reality, and there is nothing sublime about my current state of unremitting despair—all poetically or intellectually inclined people, with the unconscious, pompous dishonesty so characteristic of them, unwittingly contrive later, when their perception of hours and minutes abandons them, to invent, as it were, a sense of time, which they reconstruct (such is the case with war as it happens, as it is subsequently written down, and as it is certainly, even if inadvertently, fabricated—whether in the way of heroic deeds or humanity and kindness). Right now, I find myself caught in a vicious circle of loathsome jealous thoughts, and the keener my despair, the more obsessive and importunate these petty cares become, cheapened still by the awareness of their end, which end, granted, is perceived only in the mind, yet is as apparent as any end, as even the end of a happy, true, poetic love, no matter how we might try to idolize it and stretch it out to infinity—but what matters is to believe it boundless. The end of despair will come—in the form of disregard, ennui, replacement, perhaps even a foolish and pitiful death from exhaustion—but for now, broodingly and egotistically, I am filled with those same old calculations about Lyolya's disposition toward me, the exact, ultimate configuration of her loyalty. I incessantly register every word that she utters, every gesture, every look, even her very silences, and I compare how all this transpires with me and how she is with Bobby. I will knock, enter, and find Lyolya busy with a book or her toilette ("Oh, it's you," she will say), and, having neglected to offer me her hand, she will once again immerse herself in her interrupted activity, which is so inaccessible to me, and so vexing. But whenever Bobby comes in, she will immediately throw aside the book and ask with a smile: "Well, where shall we go, then?" These eternal comparisons and calculations of mine involve a strange combination of coldness, insight (which by now comes easily), and some feverish, almost absurd superstition: if, as I leave of an evening, Lyolya asks me distractedly, "Will you come tomorrow?" (needless to say, she will not trouble herself to listen to the answer), I feel almost relieved, for this throwaway remark will help me sleep; if, on the other hand, she says nothing, or—as is more likely, more often the case—turns only to Bobby, asking what he is doing and insisting that he come early tomorrow, I—indignant and embittered (how could she disregard my sense of self-respect so, how am I to forget this slight?)—shall remain awake for a long time yet, possibly until morning, crushed by the weight of ready declarations, those well-turned, murderous phrases that I shall never utter, and it will slip my mind that there can be no doubting whom Lyolya has favored and chosen, and that no charity on her part will fundamentally change anything. As I did during Lyolya's recent absence, I find myself constantly comparing something, and since the object of that comparison is being transferred from the realm of the imaginary into that of the real, it is all the bitterer, more painful, more indelible, and at times manifestly seems to age me. It is particularly awful to compare the degree of bodily (and not only sensual) intimacy—with Bobby everything is permitted, encouraged, while remaining forever out of reach for me. My surprise and indignation know no end: why may Bobby continually touch Lyolya's hand, button up the back of her dress, fix her hair, brush his own with her brush; why may he suddenly, on a lark, take Lyolya dancing about the room, lie down on her bed, while I am paralyzed by the memory of all her rebuffs and her unabashed, ever-ready disapproval? Besides, Lyolya is not (at least, not outwardly) as exuberant as many other women are, and she smiles with embarrassment if she dances with Bobby—as though she does so against her will—but in her gaze there often appears a misty, loathsome glimmer of real pleasure and a craving for even more of it, and this demure excitement is more dangerous than the deliberate, false defiance of simple, coarse, sometimes senseless women, and all the more dangerous for the fact that it is natural and can happen in my presence—whereas in Lyolya's presence I am paralyzed when it comes to any other woman and hence utterly defenseless. This paralysis of mine, this terror, often reaches absurd proportions: just this morning I happened to find myself alone with Lyolya, and I felt irresistibly drawn to go up to her and touch her hair, but I was sitting there, several paces away, in the armchair, with a newspaper that I was not reading, and could not bring myself to move from my spot, and so I decided that in order to take those few steps, in order to alter my position, I needed a pretext, however foolish it may be—I went out, allegedly to make a telephone call, spent a long time pacing back and forth between one staircase and another, and, when I returned, I involuntarily, awkwardly, for no reason whatsoever, pressed my lips to her hair. She remained perfectly still, declined to look up, and said sympathetically, but with a hint of contempt: "You needn't have gone on such a journey just for that." For some reason— in spite of all appearances—it strikes me that Lyolya, although temporarily distracted by Bobby, ought to have the foresight to keep me, and that she risks losing me: because of her favor—physical, demonstrable—because of somebody's (anybody's) victory over me, my attraction to her is being crippled, disfigured, diminished, destroyed (whether because a boundary has been crossed or because of my delicate, morbid sensitivity): Lyolya's allure is waning. I am lost and can no longer tell whether this unspeakable threat is true (or is it an invention of my own vengeful resentment?), whether that common trait—to give in to temptation, to the "thrill of the chase"—applies to me, or whether I am so in love that success and rejection no longer hold any meaning for me, for I shall never convince myself to fall out of love and shall always be able to distinguish between reality and self-indulgence, and that, still, how paralyzingly sweet it would be to stay with Lyolya forever, to be her husband—and hence to be at once her guardian and her lover. But if my feelings have not in fact weakened, then Lyolya's disfavor has instilled and inspires yet in me something resentful and petty, something that reveals itself in ever more diverse ways, and drives out kindness, thoughtfulness, and the immaculate sincerity of my feelings for her.

When I am alone, without Lyolya (and not only at night, in the grip of insomnia), I spend hours lustily imagining our vitriolic attempts to set the record straight, our ill-mannered yet well-founded rebukes, and, at the end of each disquisition, the irrevocable, pernicious words: "Yes, I know you well enough by now—why only kick a man who's down when you can finish him off entirely?" I have so lost my last stake in humanity that I await Bobby's inevitable departure (when he will take his father's place with Zina) with a mixture of curiosity and hope, and, in all likelihood, I should be terribly put out if Zina were suddenly to recover. Indeed, it begins to occur to me that Bobby's departure will solve my trivial differences with Lyolya, that she will wake up, as it were, from this fog and, repentant, aghast at what has gone on, return to me with a sense of shame, and that her present betrayal is in some way even to my advantage. We are often prepared to take comfort in our mistreatment by those whom we love and whom (presumably, or according to the foolish habit of trust) we suppose to love us too, and we take comfort—despite the enormous, unbearable sense of despair—not only in all manner of objectionable trivia, but occasionally in things that are far worse: it will seem to us that our relationship has not yet been broken off, but rather that some kind of right to reproach, some advantage, has been added—much like the accuser before the accused—and half-consciously we decide that the more we accumulate such curious and affronting advantages, the stronger and more confident we shall be. All this, of course, is wrong: we judge the women who have left us by putting ourselves in their place entirely, with all our love, with all the righteousness of that love, with all our suffering and our own sympathy for that suffering, and we ourselves repent for them and thereby assuage the pain they have caused us. If, however, we recall similar instances of our own gross betrayal, we shall see that either we considered them insignificant, being unhappy both with ourselves and with those whom we betrayed, preferring to hide, not to think or to pity, repenting only for show and fearing tedious, tear-filled rows, or else we were too strongly attracted by new relationships and would try to find fault with anything if only to leave and have done with all this dull obligation. In this way, by being irascible and deceitful, we ought to verify the perspective of others, for, if we do, it shall become clear to us at once that neither our own irreproachability, nor any guilt before us, is in the least useful or advantageous. And yet, the knowledge of being right, the unexpected blows after so many promises, even the very act of playing the constant, eagle-eyed, meticulous detective, refines us somehow, sharpening our insight and sensitivity, and hence petty calculations, baseness, and the bitterness of spurned, disfigured love can in fact teach us something, whereas a happy, contented love—for all its generosity and provision—is like unto wealth: it at times only coarsens us.

I am fixated with Lyolya's responsibility to me, but I do not blame Bobby for anything, and it is impossible to determine what he makes of his victory, to understand whether he loves Lyolya, whether he has come to some sort of understanding with her, whether he knows of my defeat. Never once has he broken the cycle—that of approximate words, inanely dazzling smiles, vague desires to undertake something and go somewhere—and so I make no effort to suppress my usual contempt for him, and am even glad to maintain it, glad also that it persists even in those moments of dispassion and equanimity. In vain do I strive to guess why Lyolya has such feelings for him—an enamored woman ought, nay, must be stirred by something—but I do not have a single, even slightly credible, inkling. Bobby seems to me, as so few do, to be spiritually impoverished—that is why, in all respects, he has a wretched, soon-reached limit (not only in his ability to express himself, but also in the very essence of what he says, and in the degree of his friendship and love), and the degree of affection that constitutes for others the beginning, the point of inception, is for him the ultimate achievement, which Lyolya and I undoubtedly attained. With his usual—and so very inept—deference, he will quiz me about Derval, the bourse, and business affairs, which never fails to put Lyolya's back up, and so, with the unjustness of a lover, she will refuse to forgive me for his schoolboy tone and humiliation, yet all the same she will look to me expectantly to see whether I will help him, whether I shall give him any advice: she is tormented by Bobby's proclivity for failure and outraged by my heartlessness, whereas for me this is my only means of avenging myself and bringing home to her (granted, in the most vulgar way) my unacknowledged superiority. All this mute conversation with Lyolya is exceedingly illuminating and grants me the independence and strength that I ordinarily lack in her presence. On the other hand, her power over me—because of how easy it is to offend, hurt, and torment me—is at times simply overwhelming, and every minute I must watch myself, lest I provoke her dissatisfaction or a scathing rebuke, and I dare now to speak only of what is benign, pale, and insignificant. Lyolya sees my terror, pusillanimous and unflattering as it is, and this provokes her natural loathing, the desire to be rid of me, to get shot of me, and often she will hear out something perfectly harmless—condescendingly, mockingly, perniciously—only to pounce on me with inexplicable malice, and then, satisfied now, and ever so slightly shamefaced, she conceals her remorse out of pride, is particularly cold, and only now and then—going much too far—flashes a conciliatory and, as it were, felicitous smile, certain that I shall forgive her ere long. I am so put upon, so deprived of agency, that I will sometimes begin a phrase, some thought, only to be stopped dead in my tracks by the fear of Lyolya's irony, her objection, her gaze, and have to finish it differently than I intended.

Before, such lack of agency seemed merely superficial; I believed that I knew the degree of my fall, which I myself had allowed and which was of my own making, and, hence, that I still retained some kind of inner independence, but now, more and more, I find myself changing so many of my former opinions about Lyolya and about my fear of her opinions. Lyolya's power—inadvertent yet boundless—consists in the extraordinary effect of her slightest favor or discontent, especially the latter—perhaps because she does not love me and has no desire to smooth over any grievances or misunderstandings, and I have no right to hope for such amends. All this is amplified still by the awareness of endless injustice—not in the opposition of love and indifference alone, but also in that Lyolya torments me, that she has brought, that she brings me unhappiness, whereas I am forever kind to her: in my confused, delirious fever, such "kindness"—the doing of good because of the desire to do it, persistently, consciously, soberly—appears real and tangible.

During rare moments of calm, I can see that all my accusations, my indignation, my compulsion to be so exacting, are wholly unfounded, that Lyolya is right about love, that what is happening is inevitable, maybe rightful, but even in this knowledge I still, with hidden lust, blame her for every little thing; another manifestation of love's curious inconsistency is knowing one thing yet still believing the exact opposite, believing wholeheartedly in what has been thoroughly refuted by the experience of others, as if success in love or despair never ends, and as if those who do not love us are guilty of something.

BOBBY HAS GONE away for a month—I had been patiently awaiting his departure and the undoubted changes that it would ring in Lyolya, but those changes, such as they are, have rather taken me aback: so as to provide some restitution to Lyolya's diminished stature, I resolved to assure myself of her ingenuousness and magnanimity— neither of which was in evidence either with Bobby or earlier on with me. As soon as Lyolya learned of Bobby's impending departure, her attitude toward him altered, cooled; she was clearly avoiding him, as though, having accustomed herself to depending on someone, she now feared to wind up without support and was slowly habituating herself, with unexpected selfish prudence, to Bobby's imminent absence. This new trait—precipitate inconstancy and adaptability—diminished Lyolya in my eyes, but proved fortunate for me, for who else could she rely on? I alone was within easy reach, her obvious, only possible source of support. And so I decided—owing to some not entirely absurd superstition—not to submit to her at once, and to make the violent internal rearrangement that was necessary (from bitterness to benevolence and irre-proachability) dependent on the time, the duration of our reconciliation—would it happen right away or only after Bob-by's departure? If Lyolya has the courage, if I mean enough to her, enough to cut Bobby out of the picture once and for all, I can and should "forgive" her; but if this is not the case, if Lyolya is sold on Bobby and I am but a fleeting comfort, then all is lost. I had not counted on the admittedly vague degree of loyalty that Lyolya still retained with regard to Bobby (the insufficiency of which had so infuriated me); I forgot how those treacherous words, uttered all but to his face, would have hurt him so, and I obeyed only my own, incautious, irrational sense of *amour-propre*, my age-old, violent hopes, and was sore, as though having been rejected, that my conciliatory and well-overdue conversation with Lyolya took place only this evening—a whole day after Bobby's departure—and now, in my usual pursuit of veracity and conscientiousness, I hasten to commit it to writing, lest the bitter emotional resonance of this exhausting conversation be lost or forgotten, a conversation that was again novel and more alarming than Lyolya's "confessions," revelations, and so many other exchanges over the course of our friendship, and I have—for all my fatigue, for all my desire to rest without having to think—a need to pin it down, a need that will not admit of any temptation or distraction: it is as if I have led a diary of a dangerous voyage up to a particularly gripping part—with scenes of peril and sudden, miraculous salvation— and can no longer stop myself.

I could, in fact, have had it out with her earlier, but from experience (even prior to Lyolya) I can say without reservation that nothing would have come of it, that Lyolya was too

distant and impenetrable like crystal, and so I stubbornly—
as though proving my fortitude and strength—kept silent.
Today, Lyolya drew elusively nearer, an approach that
revealed itself neither in a single word, nor in a single smile,
not until evening—in my room—when, handling me skillfully
as ever, and, intelligent and articulate as ever, she initiated the
conversation.

"It's about time that you and I had a little chat, don't you
think? The time has come for it."

"It's high time, Lyolya."

"You're unhappy with me. Tell me honestly, don't be shy."

"You won't be offended? Very well, then. I find that you're
both greedy and miserly with me." (I had prepared this in
advance.) "Greedy, because you mean to keep me, and miserly
because you won't give anything of yourself to me."

"True enough, and to the point. But if I'm greedy, that's
still to your advantage."

For all her confidence in dealing with me, however, Lyolya
spoke with difficulty, under duress, and grasped at little
things that might exculpate her, or demonstrate our insepara-
bility, or else simply flatter me.

"I knew how difficult it was for you," she continued, "but
I couldn't, I was simply too ashamed to say it."

"More's the pity—you might have helped me."

"Next time . . . No, forgive me, darling. I mustn't joke."

"How easy and pleasant it is when you aren't morose
and do joke with me." (This simply came out—doubtless

prematurely, and to my disadvantage.) "But how often have I thought that I'd never live to hear another of your friendly jokes, that I should just throw it all in."

"You mustn't think such foolish things. You're very dear to me: you know this perfectly well."

"Lyolya, if I'm so very dear to you and you wish to retain some future for us, there's an awful lot that has to be accounted for. Really, I don't understand anything anymore. You need to give me some explanations. Forgive me, but I must know what's been going on."

"Ask away."

"Are you and Bobby intimate?"

Lyolya blanched instantly; even her eyes, usually deep blue and bold, seemed to quiver and grow dim—she narrowed them slowly and lowered her head, as though unable to spit out the shameful, crucial word. I was struck by an inexpressibly uncanny feeling, and suddenly I saw all the difference in our recent situations; my mind was instantly cast back to the uncertainty and a certain hope when I suffered and lamented—insufficiently, as it turns out—and a chill ran through me when I thought about what was so terrible and yet so apparent, and what I should now have to suffer and lament: when Bobby was around, I would often imagine, with giddy, unduly sweet ecstasy, how I would catch and expose Lyolya, imagine her shame and my vindictive, mortifying departure—now there was no desire to leave, to part forever in enmity, yet all the bitterness, humiliation, and repression that had accumulated over the many months (before Lyolya's departure and during her absence) and in these cruel recent weeks—all this broke out and possessed me, supplanting my readiness to reconcile gracefully and without fuss, and so I decided in turn to torment Lyolya, to force her, however partially, to atone for her unpardonable guilt:

"When? Where? I don't understand—after all, I was always there when the two of you were at home."

"Don't ask, please. Can't you see how hard this is for me?"

"All the same, tell me as a friend—seeing that you've already forgiven my impertinent curiosity."

"If you really must know—at the Wilczewskis'."

I pictured clearly the small drawing room, and the daybed on which I had kissed Zina, and on which even yesterday Lyolya might have kissed Bobby, and I automatically thought of the strange twist of fate. Lyolya was sitting opposite me, helpless but stubborn, trying not to give in to my resentment or to stray from that initial tone of benevolent mutual sincerity. She turned to me with the utmost conviction, as though wishing to impress on me some new, unimpeachable chastity, said:

"If only you knew how unbearable it is for me—you know what I'm talking about—how I wish it wasn't a part of me. After all, it's the reason for each—yes, each and every one of my misfortunes. It's why Sergei left me back then, in Moscow, and now again . . . He told me everything: his fear, his ignorance of me, how he was sure that it would all end badly. It's why I got involved with my husband, and now with Bobby. You're an intelligent man—tell me how to change. Really, I don't want to be like this."

Lyolya's candor failed to make an impression on me: I was too preoccupied with a point of clarification, some investigative work that had yet to be completed:

"And that's all you had with Bobby—nothing noble or tender?"

She paused for a moment or two and then suddenly sat up:

"No, I would have preferred love. To you, he's a nonentity—and you aren't wrong. I know what he's worth. But doesn't it move you when some good-for-nothing suddenly shows a bit of promise? What mattered to me was that Bobby, so vacant and insignificant, raised his sights, stood on his own two feet. You don't need love like he does; you're a good sort and can stand well enough on your own."

It occurred to me that I had at last apprehended Lyolya's "idea" of love; more to the point, she did not disavow this idea, and so must love him yet.

"But you're still in love with Bobby?" (Once again, as though in confirmation and shame, Lyolya lowered her head.) "So what am I to do? How am I to return to you? Don't forget, you used to say that your greatest fear was inconstancy. Sergei taught you to fear it with his sudden departure, and now you've taught me. Just think, how can I ever feel settled with you now?"

"Yes, it's a sorry situation. I resolved to be perfectly candid, and just look how terribly it's all turned out. Women really ought to lie."

"Lyolya, you're right to be candid. The truth will always out—only, after a lie, it's so much the worse. But you can't, in the space of a single hour, do away with all the impressions that have accumulated over a whole month." (My "idea" of not exacting revenge suddenly reared its head.) "After all, it's as though you've been deliberately pushing me away this last month. You went around as if you were blind and didn't even notice the difference in generosity, and that difference doesn't come from the fact that we're different people, but rather from the fact that we treated each other differently. You ignored a thousand little things." (I would write them down at home, in a separate notebook, under the heading "Parallels," and I have often reread it, relishing the chance to compare and to place the blame squarely on Lyolya.) "Shall I give you an example? Whenever you made some observation, found some similarity, and I didn't agree with you, there would be an awkwardness, as though I had failed to understand you and you were actually right, and then you would try to cut me down to size—'how so?', 'oh, please!', 'what nonsense!'—and then you would shrug dismissively. It's a pity I can't imitate that look of triumph you always wore whenever I didn't know something—but if, on the other hand, I happened to mention something you didn't know, then you and Bobby would laugh: 'He's trying to show off his erudition.' And how many other examples of that there were."

It was a relief to air these pent-up accusations at long last, but Lyolya, it seemed, had begun to grow indignant and was now attempting to pick herself up and defend herself:

"I can assure you: I saw everything—only I couldn't see what I could do to help matters. Imagine, you have a friend who's fallen on hard times or is getting on in years—is it really possible to console him? To my mind, you oughtn't even to pity his situation with others, lest he read in their eyes those terrible words 'sympathy' and 'consolation.' Would it not be better, more considerate, simply to say nothing and thereby show him: 'Yes, you have it bad, but I know you're strong, that you can handle it yourself'?"

"It's only now that I find that I'm strong—now that Bobby's gone."

It just slipped out—just as the delight that Lyolya was joking and being sweet to me did earlier—and, yet again, it was premature and disadvantageous: all my future independence was immediately made plain—and, what was more, in the worst possible light. I decided to remind Lyolya of the advantage that I had gained, of a certain resilience that I had displayed in the case of Bobby:

"With every passing minute, you confirm to me what I saw and what I remember—namely, that you were touched by everything except me. It seems wrong of me to commend myself, but really, did I not conduct myself at times very well—better, in fact, than you and Bobby did?"

"I was annoyed with you, and even those instances of your self-restraint seemed stalely heroic—or, forgive me, my dear, simply stale."

"But it was up to you to set the tone, through your behavior to change and channel mine, to dignify it a little. Did it not occur to you that some things cannot be unsaid or undone?"

"I came here to make it up with you in all good faith, but all you're interested in doing is trying to rattle and antagonize me. Well, I won't be rattled—take that as you will. You keep asking what happened back then, why I did this or that. My answer is that it was despite myself. But that isn't enough for you, and so you're forcing me to say what you already know full well. Yes, I hated you. There you have it. It's a known condition—irritation to the point of hatred, directed against those who dare to love us, those we can't get rid of—unless we ourselves love."

A thought struck me: here was an untimely explanation for all my callousness toward Zina, after all that obliging kindness that had suddenly brightened me. Interrupting this thought, Lyolya carried on implacably explaining, indignant at my attacks and her own unspoken rebukes that had doubtless accumulated over a long period of time:

"You used to tell me to take a good look at myself. But if only you could have seen yourself, too—how unpleasant you were at times. You hounded me every minute. I could always feel that scrutiny, that detective's gaze of yours—especially if I was dancing, or if I was lying on the bed and Bobby was sitting beside me. You almost seemed to want something to happen right there in front of you. You were shameless! Bobby used to ask me, over and over again, what right you had to watch and why I allowed it. Don't forget: you were spoiling a rare and, for all that, pleasant time for me."

Then, with glaring inconsistency (as if she had been unburdened, just as I had been, of everything that was weighing her down), Lyolya, for the first time since our trip, smiled at me as she used to do, gratifyingly and knowingly—granted, she was exhausted, half-unconvinced, and distant—and, as she used to do, she embraced me tenderly—this embrace proved kinder, more real than any of our thorny accounts of the past—and just then I rediscovered those familiar, but forever alive, caresses of ours. Tired now, Lyolya gently pushed me aside:

"So, it's to be friendship—that's settled then. I'm glad. Now go home and get some sleep—you look ghastly. Starting tomorrow, I'm going to fatten you up, and you're going to do exactly as I say."

Lyolya's solicitude is a sign of my partial rehabilitation, a sign that I have reappeared, that, quite simply, she sees me. I am content and I am weary, and, in my contentment, I am curiously excited by the prospect of our future encounters—how will it be with Lyolya now, after her clarification about Bobby, after all this news, which will undoubtedly diminish her and require of me a new (perhaps censorious) kind of gentleness and pity? I recall our conversation without the least animosity—for it was the natural, long-awaited collision of Lyolya's and my truths of love: thus has it always been that the lover notices and recalls only his own love, its delights and the wrongs inflicted on it, whereas the wrongs brought to bear on another's love are forever superficial and pale in the mind and in the conscience. This is yet another proof of the diminished capacity that love results in, of the changes it rings for all human rules and relations, of the need for flexible, somewhat arbitrary, lenient laws for those in love—just as there are for children and the insane.

Now I can speak of love more soberly and soundly than usual: now begins that most pleasant part of writing, the most truthful and focused, when the resistant lull of lethargy, the temptation to dream and rest, has been overcome, when the outside world—my greatest challenge—has more or less been put to bed, when all that remains are self-evident conclusions that have long been apparent, conclusions that suggest themselves readily, matter-of-factly, and dispassionately. Long pent-up inspiration (or, more accurately, that obscure force that drives the soul, which we are granted by some miracle, out of nothingness, but which grows and spreads out infinitely, for reasons that are not in the least accidental—because of everything that has touched us or is bound to us)—and, after so many trials and errors, this unwieldy force is unleashed by me, leading me into a particular

state of mind, one that is intensely feverish, attentive to minutiae, most productive, and altogether exhausting, a state that
is doubly perturbing for the fear that I might let something
slip through my fingers forever. In this state, I can see better
what is happening to me, I can see more clearly, and often do
I correct the mistakes of my ecstatic, more exaggerative hours.
So it is that love now seems—in spite of many things that
I have previously determined—to be something mundane,
shameless, boastful, and even its non-exclusivity (that
"universality" that would sometimes move me—"everyone
remembers their beloved") now, in my sobriety, while I am
neither inebriated with drink nor intoxicated by some Gypsy
romance, diminishes love's fascinating charm, its high value,
much as the war caused so many people—because of the similar
"universality" of mortal danger and suffering—to lose their
ability to relate proportionately, rationally, properly, not only
to their own inevitable death, but also to that of others,
likewise to any illness or affliction, and also to adventure
and danger. I should find it shameful now to reread how
I worshipped at the altar of love—now, when I discover that I
have naïvely been deceived, that I in no way differ from the
"ideological" or the faithful, whom I used to mock (admittedly,
with a dash of envy) from on high—but my disappointment
does not lie in Lyolya, who has proved worse than I imagined,
nor in her lack of reciprocity, nor even in that all love is
changeable, finite, and within reach of a nobody like Bobby,
but rather it lies in one thing alone, something that struck me

suddenly, intensely, irrevocably: like everything we know, like faith and the noble ideals for which we sacrifice ourselves, love is here, among us, not on the other side, but on this side, in this world, and love will not reveal to us that other world— undoubted though impenetrable—nor can it ever do so.

It is impossible to live without deceit, however: we are made so that we shall never find our way out of this dead end, and, amid the other ever-present contradictions that seem to mock us is the need for deceit, at the very least for an errone- ous, arbitrary conjecture, or, more precisely, for that curious mental exertion that can be produced only by deception, and from which alone derives that most intriguing, most inexplicable activity of ours—shaking off the desolate human darkness, extracting more and more fragments of indisput- able knowledge. Without this, there can be only ordinary, everyday, loathsome, impotent ennui, or else an icy sense of elation that is blind to both time and people and constitutes a living death. Yet it so happens that I have within me a surfeit of ardor, enthusiasm, life's fullness, a reserve that leads— through my devotion to love, through my attempts to idolize it—to an awareness of deceit, its necessity, and its inevita- bility, an instinct that is equipped with a sufficient degree of circumspection and that has tempered and refined itself: I must find a use for it, I must, in reckoning with a fate that has already been determined, direct my enthusiasm unerringly— not in the pursuit of happiness (which is a gift and a miracle), but for the sake of the individual's struggle with blindness, or so that this obscure, doomed, lofty struggle shall be visible. Any human transcendence—whether it be lovingly idealistic and self-sacrificing or achieved through faith—provided that it does not become a wonted, stagnant duty, is a kind of ardor that is cooled, only for it continually to re-emerge somewhere, and it is a genuine ardor, one that we cannot replace and cannot force. To descend, to fly off and not attain some new transcendence, is impossible, and since other possible attempts have been killed by my natural ineptitude, by some unforgettable and crushing blow, I will not mortify the only possibility that remains: if I have been given no other pinnacle than love, and no other love than Lyolya, and if love, as well as any pinnacle, is but a deception, and Lyolya embodies deceit, and if today, alone with her, without any rival, in the moment of my most passionate hope, she has definitively pushed me away, then I shall not run away, nor shall I repress anything inside me, but rather I shall offer up my already dwindling strength to the cruel and fertile whims of love's divinity, to the god of love who has never forsaken me, nor yet claimed my victory. One could easily suspect that all this is a game, that I am embellishing and, as it were, crafting an artificial love, or, on the contrary, that I am contriving clever arguments lest I pluck out my beating love for Lyolya, but then it is I who must suffer because of this love, I who must wait for Lyolya's uncomprehending callousness, who must horribly and irreparably debase myself before her, who must depend on Bobby and on absurd external circumstances, I who must witness their intolerable power, at night, in the midst of insomnia, I who must curse my suicidal triviality and, in my improbable nightly fantasies, disfigure and blacken that same Lyolya for whom all this was begun and endured; what's more, experience has taught me to prepare for the worst when the going is good, and that I shall find no good in the bad—more than that, that I have a sense of honor like any other man, and that I do not have any special aptitude for self-edification, that a reciprocated earthly love is, I believe, the most worthy and beautiful kind of love, and that the first pain will come the very moment the work distracting you from that love ends—such a hopeless choice is not a sophistry, nor is it a pose or a game, but an attempt to remain true (even amid misfortune) to some human purpose, perhaps misunderstood, but binding me all the same, if I am to understand it in this way, and can find no fault in such understanding.

Acknowledgments
and a dedication

The poet and novelist Boris Poplavsky once described literature as an act of friendship. "Art is a private letter sent at
random to friends unknown," he declared in 1932 in the essay
Amid Doubt and Evidence. "It's a kind of protest against the
separation of lovers in space and time." Poplavsky, another
Parisian émigré and a good friend of Yuri Felsen's, knew what
he was talking about.

When I first came across Felsen's work almost a decade
ago, he instantly found a sympathetic friend, although it has
taken some considerable time for that friendship to bear the
fruit of this translation. During that time, I have incurred, on
the long and tortuous path to publication, several debts of
friendship, which I hope to repay here, if only in part.

To the living descendants of Felsen, who so willingly
shared with me their family history and shone a distant,
unexpected light on Felsen's life, I offer up this book, hoping to give you your first glimpse of a relative you ought to
have known but whom the evils of his age took away before

his time. Bright be his memory, and may that memory be a blessing.

I should also like to thank Ben Schrank and Signe Swanson at Astra House, two of Felsen's newest friends, and the rest of the team at Astra for placing their faith in me and responding so positively to this work from the moment they encountered it. It is a privilege to be able bring Felsen's *Deceit* to new audiences with your support.

Likewise, this publication would not have been possible without the charitable support of the Mikhail Prokhorov Foundation and its TRANSCRIPT program, which allowed me to undertake this first major translation of Felsen's work. The foundation's generosity has enabled this silenced voice to speak anew in our world today.

To Anastasia Tolstoy and Dzmitry Suslau, both of whom offered much too freely of their time, patience, and expertise in reading various drafts of this work, I owe a lasting debt of gratitude. Your unstinting generosity has at times, I fear, been both a testament to and a test of our friendship.

My final words of acknowledgment bring me to a dedication. To the late Ivan Juritz, with whom I shared my early enthusiasm for Felsen, I say this: In translating *Deceit* alone, and not with you, I have missed your wit, your imagination—in a word, your genius. Yet your still-lingering friendship has sustained and guided me through every word. This book is for you.

ABOUT THE AUTHOR

Yuri Felsen was the pseudonym of Nikolai Freudenstein. Born
in St. Petersburg in 1894, he emigrated in the wake of the Russian Revolution, first to Riga and then to Berlin, before finally
settling in Paris in 1923. In France, he became one of the leading writers of his generation, alongside the likes of Vladimir
Nabokov; influenced by the great modernists such as Marcel
Proust, James Joyce, and Virginia Woolf, his writing stood at
the forefront of aesthetic and philosophical currents in European literature. Following the German occupation of France at
the height of his career, Felsen tried to escape to Switzerland;
however, he was caught, arrested, and interned in Drancy concentration camp. He was deported in 1943 and killed in the
gas chambers at Auschwitz. After his death he fell into obscurity and his work is only now being translated into English.

ABOUT THE TRANSLATOR

Bryan Karetnyk is a British writer and translator. His recent translations include works by Gaito Gazdanov, Irina Odoevtseva, and Boris Poplavsky. He is also the editor of the landmark Penguin Classics anthology *Russian Émigré Short Stories from Bunin to Yanovsky*.